SPACE TRUCKERS

MOTHER LOAD

B.C. DUTOUR

To order additional copies of this book, contact:
Gotham Books
1- 307-464-7800
www.gothambooksinc.com

PART ONE

THE MIDAS TOUCH

I OPEN MY EYES AND stare at the unopened email file blinking across my hotel room's computer screen. I must have dozed off at the computer desk because I don't recall getting this info, which is now two hours old. 'Damn!' I thought to myself. 'When did I fall asleep?' I remember the last thing I was at a popular cafe, for starship captains only, called the Ready Room. It was on Fisherman's Wharf, floating in the San Francisco Bay and I was drinking some very good tea. I had sat there all morning waiting for the fog to clear which is now the fog of war. As I sat there musing, I thought I could get one last good look at the Golden Gate Bridge and Alcatraz Prison in the noon day sun while I waited for the shuttle that would take me to my final destination, my hotel room at the Stanley Park Imperial Chateau in what was once the country of Canada. Yes, the park is now a resort and hotel.

After the Emperor attacked earth, the Emperor's Collective tried to preserve as much of the park as they could by building a biodome over the park and erecting two hotel towers around the lush forest. What can I say, Stanley Park is still beautiful and so is Fisherman's Wharf. I click on the attached file and this is what glares back at me.

From Nova-Tech Laboratories and Logistics Corporation. RE: Jaycen Vollmer Dispatcher. To Captain Jonathan Archibald Mott, of the Nova-Tech star freighter Supernova.

Just to inform you that the labour dispute is now in negotiations, there is still no word on how long this will take, so you will have to make do without any engineers for now.

Maintenance crews are also making a fuss, and are now saying. "If ship engineers are on strike so, are we, after all, we belong to the same union." Isn't that some B.S? Eh!

'That's just great!' I thought to my self. 'No engineers, B.S. Is right!' 'And those lazy goods for nothing maintenance crews!' Bloody hell, you guys!' I keep reading the file.

Your ship is waiting for you in orbit, at docking bay eighty-seven. Your cargo is food and medical supplies destined for Orion Station. Welcome back. I hope your vacation went well. Safe travels Jaycen.

Also attached to this file is a bill of lading that I upload to my command node, a small powerful multi-functional device that I wear on my wrist. Once done my morning routine I gather my personal effects and head down to the lobby and the cab waiting outside. When inside the taxi I order the Cabby to take me to the spaceport. The waiting shuttle there will take me to docking bay eighty-seven and my ship the Supernova, moored in orbit at Earth Docks.

Finally, after forty-five minutes, which seemed to take longer because the cabbie just would not shut up, I breathed a sigh of relief and headed into the shuttle that will take me to the docks orbiting Earth. Another two hours of flight time jostles you around to a point of near panic because it feels like the whole freakin' shuttle is going to be ripped apart by the g-forces of leaving Earth's gravity. Once outside the Earth's stratosphere, it's a smooth ride. Meanwhile, this entire ride is brought to you by the elegant sounds of Max Weight and The Moose Whistles. like elevator music is going to calm your near panic experience, what the hell!

I wake up as the shuttle gets near docking bay eighty-seven, two hours later. I smile as I see a massive structure that looms ahead. 'There she is.' I thought to myself. 'The Supernova, my ship.' Here's the thing, to describe the Supernova as a large star freighter you'd be doing an injustice, she's not just a large freighter she is colossal in size. In fact, the Supernova is a colossus class star freighter, one of three to be exact. Although the dimensions of each one vary, Supernova's dimensions, however, make her the largest of her kind.

These are the dimensions. From bow to stern, the length is fifteen kilometers, from the port, to starboard the width is two point five kilometers, and within the hull of my lady are decks going three kilometers from top to bottom which dwarfs the tallest buildings on Earth. The ship is so large, it has twenty-seven cargo bays and one gigantic hangar bay which is two point five kilometers long by two point five kilometers wide and one kilometer high. The Supernova's main engines are also massive and are capable of faster than light speed or warp speed.

Ok, let me clarify something, the term warp is what we space Ferrers use to determine speeds at faster than light speed, or F.T.L. It is also a physical state, at which a ship enters F.T.L. Flight from point A to point B. It is in this state that time and space seem to physically warp around you, hence the term warp speed. With engines as massive as they are you might think going top F.T.L. or high warp would be no problem and you'd probably be right, but the Supernova is not meant for Top F.T.L. only a low warp. The size of the Supernova is the reason we dare not exceed warp five. It's because of all the space debris that gets sucked at the moment we jump to faster than light speeds.

The event horizon that is caused by a ship going from real space to warp space as some now call it, creates some kind of a wake or current or undertow, etc, etc, that pulls all kinds of debris with it. This debris is now traveling faster than light and cannot slow down or come out of the warp.

Now that humanity has gone three millennia traveling the cosmic highway at faster than light speeds, all kinds of junk pose a threat to the superstructure of the Supernova, therefore we travel at a low F.T.L. It's so we can maneuver our behemoth ship and avoid the larger crap that's out there in the warp.

The Supernova is also a local vessel and must not exceed the sol's system speed limit of warp three, which is fine by me and it is set by and enforced by none other than the C.H.I.M.P.S. Or chimps as I call them and they are the Cosmic, Highway, Intergalactic, Magistrate, Police, Service. Whew, that's a mouth full, chimps so much easier to say. I love this ship and I'm the one in charge and my name is Captain John Mott.

A little while later I'm in my ready room located beside the bridge. I was logging in to the ship's computer systems at my desk when no sooner had I arrived and already I'm interrupted by a crew member. "What!" I yell, no response, again the door chimes indicating a crew member wants to talk. "Come in!" And yet again the door chimes. I hustle across the room and growl. "For the love of the cosmos!" I hit the door button. "Swoosh!" the door slides open, I peered out into the corridor and nary a soul was seen. 'That's just great, let the shenanigans begin!' I thought out loud in frustration. 'Frikken ice holes!'

Log entry #1. Start of an 8hr shift. 0800 hrs. It's now been two weeks since we left Earth Docks for Orion Station and a whole mess of problems have occurred. The first thing to happen is the main turbo thrusters are offline, without these special thrusters working we can't jump to F.T.L. And make matters worse we don't know what the problem is because no one on board the Supernova is certified to diagnose or repair the engines. Without engineers on board because of the labour dispute we are left to circumnavigate the stars by our hypersonic enertia and docking thrusters. Also, our Orillian Patron, Lord Holland Monical, knew we had no engineers on the ship, but that didn't matter to him, for an additional cost one can get the engineering staff of any major port, like Earth Docks, to prep a ship for hypersonic velocity and an F.T.L. Jump. And away we went. My theory is that Lord Monical just wanted us gone and didn't bother to pay for the F.T.L. Jump.

The second thing to happen is one of my bridge crew has been spreading rumors that the ship is haunted. It's because of all the glitches that have been going on, like my door chime, no maintenance is being done either. Truth is a ship these large needs round-the-clock maintenance. Bloody labour dispute! And do you know what gets me? The rest of the bridge crew now thinks the ship is haunted too. I know who it is. You see, I've got a crew member who likes to play practical jokes and I know to whom he said it first. My communications officer. I'll reprimand this crewman when I can prove it.

Once again, my door chimes. "Come in!" I project from across my desk. "Swoosh!" The door to my ready room slides open. And to my relief in walks one of my bridge officers.

"Sir if you're done with your logbook we need you on the bridge a-sap."

"What's the problem Lieutenant?" I ask as I close out my logbook.

"Well sir we received a distress signal and Commander Crane wants to know if you want to check it out?"

"Alright, I'm coming," I say as I get up from my desk and follow my crewman out the door. I start to think as I make my way to the bridge. 'I leave my first officer in charge, while I'm working on my logbook and he still can't make his own decisions. My ship has the worst bridge crew ever, even slackers would say they are slackers.'

I arrive on the bridge a moment later to find the usual faces staring blankly at me. Commander James Crane A.K.A. Cranky, my first officer, is old enough to be my grandfather. Grey hair, trimmed white beard. Should be ship's captain. He's been the first mate of the Supernova since I came aboard twenty years ago. He says he hates change and likes being the first officer. And his ice blue eyes are as cold as his demeanor.

Then there's Acting Sub Lieutenant Don Watts our helmsman, this kid can fly this bucket of bolts through an ion storm and won't scratch any paint. As for personality, well he's got about as much personality as a jug of water. He has mousy coloured hair and the dour look in his grey eyes are a constant thing. The pale color of his skin is also a match for his personality as well.

Next is Lieutenant Commander Lee Oswald, this enormous augmented human is head of my security, he had some kind of top-secret military training and says he's done a couple of tours of duty in the ongoing colony war, a bit on that a little later. He is tall with blond hair and his blue eyes are a bit fidgety. He's always pulling his blaster gun and pointing it down the hallways, saying he saw something. Sometimes he jumps up from his seat startling us, as he dashes off down one of the corridors waving his gun in the air. One time he even shot his blaster gun and that was the only time we had an android on board. We had not been in space for more than a week when the guy blew a hole through the androids' heads.

Then there's our navigations officer, Lieutenant Charles Vollmer brother of Jaycen Vollmer our company dispatcher. Well, what can I say he's the brother of a dispatcher kind of like two peas in a pod if I do say so myself. Not much to tell about him either he is fairly tall and quite skinny he also has reddish colored hair and green eyes and he is good at his job, and only good.

Next is the bridge's science officer Lieutenant Leon Fernandez, this guy is probably the only normal guy on this space boat besides me of course. However, I would say he's normal if it weren't for the fact that he sports a purple mohawk on his tanned head and listens to ancient music from the late twentieth century called punk rock. He is average in height and his dark brown eyes very much portray his intelligence.

Then there is Lieutenant Robert or "Bob" Thompson, the guy that came and got me, from my paperwork, has no real title, he thinks he is a lieutenant but actually isn't. He is the son in law of our boss, Lord Holland Monical. His Lordship told me to keep an eye on him, so I gave him a commision on the bridge. Much to the dismay of the other bridge crew, they don't think it's fair, frankly I don't either we all had to earn our commissions. Also he likes to play practical jokes at other people's expense, like telling my communications officer that the ship is haunted. No one on board the Supernova likes him, no matter how many times we tell him to stop, he won't. I think that's why he's here, Lord Monical doesn't like him either. So we're stuck with the guy, for now. As for his looks well he is quite homely looking, his brown hair and light brown eyes don't improve his looks either. How he managed to be married to a daughter of a lord is beyond me.

And last but not least, is Lieutenant Marvin "The Martian" Lewinsky, my communications officer. This guy is so paranoid he thinks aliens abducted all of us, probed us, and now he's quite convinced the aliens did unthinkable acts to us while we were unconscious too. Then they beamed us back to the Supernova and they are now monitoring us from our communications array. Also he is the one that convinced the crew that the ship is haunted thanks to Bob. Marvin is also average in height with dark almost black hair.

Where Leon's eyes reflect his intelligence, Marvin's deep blue eyes betray his.

One thing they have that the other captains don't in this fleet, is loyalty. They just won't leave no matter what happens and they respect me more than anyone else in their lives, and that makes them able to work well together, most of the time. Finally I'm noticed once I'm half way across the bridge.

"Ah, Skipper, kept your chair warm for ya I did." Said my first officer as I approached the command station on board the bridge of the Supernova.

"Smells like your ass Cranky" I joke. As I slip into my chair atop its daios.

"You wish it did." chibed the first mate. "Any way Skipper we received a distress signal and wonder if ya like to investigate?"

"I've just been briefed on it by Bob and I think we should investigate, they might have non union personnel that might be able to diagnose our engine problem and do some routine maintenance around the ship."

"Very good sir I was thinking the same thing but I wanted your opinion first."

"Cranky you know as well as I do that's it's the law, you shoulda just, plotted a course for the distress signal."

"Well, Skipper if ya don't mind I got a course to plot, now slide your ass back off the command chair."

"Ha ha funny old man just get it done, and that's an order Commander. On second thought, I'll do it, after all it was you that brought me out here in the first place. Charles plot a course to the distress signal, and Don, engage once you receive the new course heading."

"Yes captain!" they both said together.

"Charles what's our E.T.A. for Orion Station?" I ask my navigation officer.

"Uhm lets see at our current rate of speed six months and eleven days, shouldn't we tell dispatch about this?" He asks turning around in his seat to look at me.

"No not yet, what's the E.T.A. for the distress signal." I continue.

"Let's see, approximately five hours." Said my navigation officer turning back around to look at his monitor again.

"Don is the new course laid in yet?" I demand.

"En route now Captain." said my helmsman.

"Good, Marvin play back the distress signal."

"Captain it's not a vocalized message it came over the medical alert frequency, it's just nav points and an S.O.S. readout." Said my communications officer.

"Frack! Must be worse than I thought." I said rubbing my chin with some measure of concern. "Well there's nothing we can do about it till we get there so in the meantime I'll be in my ready room finishing my paper work and talking to dispatch, notify me when we arrive."

"Eye, eye Captain." said the crew together.

I slipped off my chair and turn to Cranky "You have the bridge number one." I say in my best Patrick Stewart. I don't think my first officer will get the reference he's not a classic TV buff like some of the crew and myself are. I was now making my way to my office when a thought occurred to me. 'It never ceases to amaze me that a crew that has been together as long as mine has, still can't think for themselves, and my first officer can't take charge of so small a decision as to investigate an S.O.S. It's like I'm in charge of a bunch of kids, what the hell!'

It must of been the door chime or the yelling on the bridge that woke me five hours later. "Yawn!" "What is it?" I say while stretching my arms

"Uh Captain, we are at the rescue coordinates."

"Thanks Bob, I'll be on the bridge in a minute!" Well dispatch told me to go ahead with the rescue too, Jaycen, was thinking about non union maintenance and engineer crews as well. Truth be told I didn't have to be asked by anybody to go ahead with a rescue, it was law, if there's a distress signal from somewhere, the nearest ship must investigate and the Supernova is the nearest ship.

I arrive on the bridge a few minutes later and an argument with Cranky and Charles was going on, something about the nav-points being wrong. As usual this wouldn't be the first time Cranky was yelling at someone, hence the name Cranky.

"Alright already, stop yelling, for crying out loud!" "Guys, I don't want to be interrupted from my paperwork by your arguing all the time!" I chastise, as I make my way across the bridge to where the argument is taking place.

"Ok, what's the matter?" 'Kids, I thought to myself, daddy's here now we can all play nice.'

"Skipper there is nothing out there but a bunch of asteroids, Charles must of got the nav-points mixed up again." Said Cranky accusingly.

"No way man you always blame me! I did not make a mistake, the nav-points are totally correct!" Argued Charles Vollmer in return.

"Ok, ok, take it easy, you know you have gotten them wrong before." I say looking down at my navigations officer and folding my arms with an air of authority.

"Holy cow really, it was one time, am I never going to hear the end of it?"

"Just calm down and show me ok."

"Fine."

Charles shows me his navigation screen and continues talking. "See, this is the S.O.S. read out from Marvin's screen to mine, the nav-points are the same, latitude forty five degrees, longitude ten degrees destination point zero, six, five, three, dash A. Both screens are a match."

"It's the same on mine as well." Said Helmsman Don Watts.

"Ok, so where's the ship?" I ask somewhat puzzled as I look over to the heads up display and view empty space and asteroids.

"Good question Skipper, we have been trying to figure that one out for the past ten minutes." Said Cranky the ships commander, looking at empty space and asteroids too in the heads up display.

As we were all trying to find an explanation as to why there was no ship to rescue a great explosion ruptured throughout the big freighter knocking us about like ragdolls.

"What the hell was that?" I barked, picking myself off the floor.

"Sir!" Said Lee Oswald as he climbed back to his station. "My computer tells me we've just been fired upon by a proton torpedo and our shields are out."

"What! I cry out as I slide into my chair. "We don't have the shield capacity for that kind of impact, our shields are only meant for small asteroids and backing into loading docks!"

"I know Captain." Said Lee.

"Ok Lee run a sensor scan and find out who shot the proton torpedo at us!" I order.

"Right away Captain." Obeyd Lieutenant Commander Lee Oswald.

"Uh Captain we've…."

"Not now Marvin I don't have time for your conspiracy theories. Lee also find out how much damage there is?"

"I already know Captain."

"Well, let's hear it then." I demand.

"Decks one through five, aft of the hangar bay has no power, the impact must've knocked the power units out in that area. Also cargo bays twenty to twenty five are destroyed all damage was centred there."

"Any injuries? Deaths?" I inquire.

"None sir, reports are coming in from around the ship saying no one is injured or dead and that no one was scheduled for cargo inspection at the time of impact." Replies my head of security.

"Thank the stars for that," I said a little relieved.

"Uh Captain?"

"Not now Marvin! Lee what does the sensor scans say?"

"Scans say there is no ship in the area but ours and the only thing in this area other than our ship is a very large asteroid and a billion smaller ones."

"So who the hell fired the proton torpedo?" I asked scratching my head in puzzlement.

"I don't know and neither does the computer." Answers Lee Oswald, gesturing toward his computer screen.

"Great I've got a huge hole in the side of my ship, cargo spilling out, and a mysterious torpedo from nowhere caused it! What next?" I demand to no one in particular while crossing my arms in frustration.

"How about we let the pirates um I don't know, take the ship like they asked a few minutes ago, well it's more like demanded." Answers Lieutenant Marvin Lewinsky communications officer of the Nova-Tech Laboratories and Logistics Corporation space freighter known as the Supernova.

"What pirates?" We all demand together.

"The pirates that hailed us after the explosion, I tried telling you Captain but you wouldn't listen to me." Said my communications officer a little annoyed at being ignored.

"Marvin, this better not be one of your conspiracy theories!" I say pointing an accusing finger in his direction.

"No Captain it's not do you want me to play the message or not?"

"Yes Marvin play it."

"Eye, eye,… Captain."

And this is what the message said…

…Starfreighter Supernova this is Admiral Victor Kruel, leader of Midas Eighty-Eight. We want your ship, furthermore we know you don't have any shields left and any attempt to flee will result in your total annihilation. You have one hour to comply or we open fire again…

"Captain they also left their hailing frequency open so we can comply. Do you want me to return a message?"

"No not yet Marv, Commander Crane will tell you when." I look over to Cranky and give him a sly smile and he just shakes his head as I resume talking with my communications officer. "First triangulate sensor scans from Lee's consul to the comm array and pinpoint the exact location of where this message came from. I want to know where these pirates are."

"Roger that, ok done." Said my communications officer a moment later.

"Now give me the location based on the transmission." I order.

"Wow, according to these readings Captain the transmission came from the giant asteroid." Said Lieutenant Marvin Lewinsky in amazement.

"Captain I found something else." Said science officer Lieutenant Leon Fernandez.

"What is it Leon?" I ask.

"I also triangulated scans based on scientific analysis and that giant asteroid is one colossal gold nugget and a mining colony as well."

I whistle, out my surprise and continue my discussion with the bridge crew. "So these pirates must of found out about the asteroid being solid gold and took the colony by force, sent out a fake distress signal to lure an unsuspecting ship and then use the planetary defences against said ship, which happen to be us."

"That would be my guess too Captain." Replies L.T. Leon Fernandez while he was typing frantically on his computer console.

In keeping with the conversation, my helmsman, Don Watts, upset with the news interrupted. "The colony is just miners and their families, they wouldn't of stood a chance against armed pirates. I hope they are ok?"

"Ya me too Son, me too." I say in empathy.

"There's just one thing I'm having a problem rapping my finger around Captain." Says Bob Thompson wanting to be a part of the conversation for once.

"Ya what's that Bob?"

"How did the pirates get there? I mean they don't even have a ship and they're threatening to take ours by force."

"Well, well, look who has decided to be a part of the crew after all." Commented Commander James Crane A.K.A. Cranky, with an air of sarcasm.

"Knock it off Commander now's not the time. And right you are Bob. I think I know who it is that's taken the colony by force. Anyone care to guess?" The crew just stares at me dumbfounded waiting for me to reply, I sigh and rub my face in frustration. "I'll give you all a hint, who would have access to weapons?"

"Oh, the security force of the colony they say together, then they smile and nod to one another like they just solved the greatest mystery in the universe.

I just shake my head in utter bewilderment and change the subject. "So who would actually be in charge down there would it be the security force or the corporation?" I Comment to know one in particular.

"It's the pirates now." Uttered Bob under his breath.

I shoot Bob a stern look and this was when we all found out about the giant gold asteroid and the mining colony from my science officer Lieutenant Leon Fernandez.

"Captain, I was searching the net for more info on recently found giant gold asteroids, and I found out there's one called Midas Eighty Eight and that is exactly what we are looking at now, Midas Eighty Eight. It was discovered by an astrogeologist named DR. Roger Midal. The good doctor was given a government grant by the former federation to survey the asteroid field for sources of helium three and that's when he happened upon the giant gold asteroid and aptly named it Midas Eighty Eight."

There was more of Leon's blather, but I chose to ignore him at that moment to access the info from his computer console via my command node on my wrist and it appeared instantly on the bridges heads up display, or "hud" as we call it. There was even a picture of the good doctor. He was what you'd expect of a scientist, older man with thick glasses, balding, wearing a white lab coat. "Doesn't seem the type to be doing field work." I interrupt. "He looks too old for that kind of labour."

Leon turns around in his chair and gives me a contemptuous look, and blurts out "Are you finished?"

"Yup." I say with a look of my own, and my science officer continues.

"As I was saying the doctor owns the rights to this asteroid and he started a mining corporation and built the colony on said asteroid. There you have it Captain, the answer to your question, the doctor is the one in charge."

This was when Cranky piped in.

"It does not seem likely that the good doctor is in charge, he may own it all and I would wager he does not know the first thing about running an entire colony, that duty would fall to the Planetary Governor. This person is a politician and he or she, may or may not work for the corporation. But they most definitely work for the former federation. That being said this person is also the one to have the colonies best interest in mind. Making sure the civilians are, fed, clothed, housed and have jobs to do. The safety of the colony is the resposibility of the F.A.F. You know, the Federal Armed Forces and I have know Idea if the empire has moved in or not because the info Lieutenant Fernandez got for us is twenty years old.

I look over at Leon and shrug my shoulders in a disappointed gesture and he just shrugs back. I then return back to the conversation gawking at the good Doctor's picture yet again. That's a big responsibility for one person to try and keep order over the People and the F.A.F. Maybe even the forces of the new empire too. I say.

'Yes Indeed Captain. Of course, he or she would have an entire administration to help them and their own security as well, we are after all living tumultuous times. Continued Cranky. "A place like this Captain is a country unto itself, He continued. It would have a market, hospital, school, security barracks, administration building, public library, law offices, warehouses, sewage treatment plants, smelters, mines and of course housing. Oh and also a major space port and logistics centre."

"Ok Commander we are getting off track, now then, we've determined that the pirates are the local law enforcement, and probably have there own families down there too."

"Some of them Captain but not all of them." Said Commander James Crane.

"At any rate, these are people who swore to uphold the law and protect the community. Just what the hell went on down there?" I ask with concern and frustration.

"Well something went on down there and it is bad really bad." Replies Cranky with as much concern in his voice as mine.

"Your right Commander, it is bad and I aim to find out just what the hell happened down there. Because there is not supposed to be any problems on a galactic colony. Lee I have a job opportunity for ya one that requires military training what do you say are you up for an away mission?"

"Yes Sir, now you're talking my language." Said the security officer enthusiastically. "What do you have in mind Captain?"

"I'll tell you in a minute, what I want you to do. That being said, it has come to my attention that when you arrived on this ship from your vacation on Earth, you brought with you quite the arsenal of weapons?"

"I, I… Uh, I don't know what you're talking about Sir." Replied Lieutenant Commander Lee Oswald looking down at his computer console and fidgeting apprehensively.

"Don't gimme that!" I said pointing an accusing finger. "Every day since we've left Earth Docks you arrive on the bridge with a new gun in your holster, and just the other day I noticed you had an assault rifle strapped to your back. So don't play coy with me, Lieutenant Commander." I smirk as I lean back in my chair and continue. "Frankly I think it's great that you have all those weapons stashed in your quarters because it's times like this that were going to need them."

"So, you're not mad then?"

"Hell no, what you've done Lee is given us a means to protect ourselves, we are now in a hostile area that has gone unnoticed and this is the first we've heard of Midas Eighty Eight." Now my attention is on the entire crew. "For all we know this could be an I.R.F. Stronghold as well." I'll get to the I.R.F. in a bit.

Again Cranky comments. "That is a lot of gold these pirates are guarding."

"I know, and they just blew a hole in the side of my ship." I say glancing at the aged Commander. "If these pirates happen to be I.R.F." I let that statement soak in a nanosecond before I continued. "We may be forced to engage in combat and they've already sent us there message. Leon didn't you say that Doctor Midal was funded by the former federation?" I inquire totally captivated by the image of Midas Eighty Eight in the hud now.

"Yes I did Captain."

"So it stands to reason that this could very well be an I.R.F. stronghold we are looking at.

"Frack, I hadn't thought of that." Said the science officer realising the implications of the situation now.

"Are you sure you want to go down there Skipper? Said Cranky with concern.

"Yes I do Commander. This is still an S.O.S. And as far as I'm concerned, there are a lot of innocent people down there that need our help and thanks to our little investigation and Lee's love of weapons we might just be able to go in, rescue the civilians and have the protection we need in case hostilities arise. So then." I say turning to the bridge crew now. "Who wants to show these pirates what happens when you blow a hole in the side of our beloved ship?"

Then the entire bridge crew raised their hands up in the air like excited school children.

"I love your enthusiasm but unfortunately not all of you are going on this away mission." And just like that they slowly lowered their hands and the bridge once again fell silent. "So then, lets formulate a plan." and still they remain silent just staring at me. 'Great I've got to do it myself.' I thought. "Ok here's my plan, Lee I'm going to give you access to the personnel files which you probably should've had already, being head of my security and all, you really should know the backgrounds of all the crew on board the Supernova. I want you to do just that look at all the crew's files and find out who has military experience and recruit them for this away mission."

"Captain What if some of them are from maintenance?" Asked Lee Oswald Lieutenant Commander of the starfreighter known as the Supernova.

"Then recruit them and promote them to be your security personnel as well." And if they put up a fuss tell them they will get danger pay if they go on this away mission. Cranky looks at me in surprise and mutters something under his breath. I keep talking. "When we get to Orion Station I'll make all the promotions official." Cranky then shook his head in disapproval. 'Like I need anybody's opinion, especially his, he can't even think for himself half the time.' I thought with a look of my own. I return my attention back to Lee Oswald and continue. "Once you've got your people sorted out rally them up in the hangar bay, at my Falcon, I'll see you down there shortly, you have your orders now get to it." I command, slipping, off my chair.

"Aye aye Skipper, Said the Lieutenant Commander, saluting me enthusiastically. then he realised his mistake and cringed.

"Hey!" I snapped, pointing my finger at Lee. "No one calls me Skipper except Cranky and no one calls him Cranky but me, guys we've been through this a million times, I say pointing my finger at the bridge crew with a little disdain in my eye.

"Yes Captain." The crew says together turning their chairs around slowly and hanging their heads.

I saw a couple of junior crew men whispering something just then and my attention was averted, I call out from across the bridge as my pointing finger fell on them "Got something to add Jaywalkers?" The two of them were making there way to the turbo lift and froze.

These junior crew men, or Jaywalkers as I call them are the responsibility of one Miss Samantha Crane the granddaughter of our beloved first officer. Cranky brought her aboard the Supernova because her parents died in the colony war that our so called, benevolent Emperor currently wages. That's the reason I like to think she's here. There is another other reason as well and it's more political in its intrigue. You see, Samantha Crane is another captain, albeit a junior class captain, but a captain nonetheless. Cranky that old fool brought her on board without telling me about her rank and I haven't been able to figure out why. I do have a theorie, which involves military training but every time I try to bring up her file, I get an access denied, and when I question her about her file she just shrugs her shoulders and says she doesn't know why I can't access the info. Her file is the only one on this entire ship no one can access, not even my two best hackers, Leon Fernandez and Marvin Lewinsky can access her file.

It's true that her parents died in the colony war and that's the excuse both Cranky and Samantha gives me for her reason to be here. So why didn't they tell me about her captain's rank? I know they're hiding something and that irks me. Mark my words I will find out the truth eventually, I always do.

The day I found out about Samantha's rank though, was the day I demoted her to the rank of commander. I also put her in charge of the night shift which was my shift, much to her dismay, of course, but I don't care, there is only room for one captain on this ship and that's yours truly. I don't think she's going to forgive me any time soon, and like I said I don't care, this is my ship, if she wants her captaincy back she is going to have to get her own ship.

Be that as it may, Samantha has not yet left, and probably won't either. She's also always telling a couple of junior bridge officers to stay after their shift in the hopes of getting intel on what's happening during the day. Normally, I just ignore them, but not today.

"Well spit it out Jaywalkers, got something to add?"

"No Captain we were just leaving," replied one of the junior officers like a frightened school child.

"No you're not!" Now the bridge went silent. "In my ready room, I'll deal with you two idiots in a few minutes. Marvin, patch Miss Crane on comms to my ready room and put her on standby. I'm standing behind my communications officer now and I can see its making him nervous.

"Mmmiss Crane is on standby Captain."

"Good, she can wait till I'm done, now patch me in to the Chief of maintenance pronto Lieutenant we need to fix that hole a-sap."

"Yes Sir, you are now patched in, go ahead Captain."

I lean down, grab the mic and thumb the switch, I hear static at first and then a guttural voice. "This is Chief Anthony Florin, speaking."

"Tony, Captain Mott here."

"Oh hey John, to what do I owe this pleasure?" Said the Chief with a hint of sarcasm.

I choose to ignore it. "I don't know if you are aware or not and seems to me like you don't want to send me any maintenance reports from around the ship or do any work, so I just thought I would see if you, heard or felt an explosion a few minutes ago?"

"Ya I did, what was that? Wrecked my card game, and I was on a winning hand too."

"Good, I'm glad that's all that got wrecked." I also said with sarcasm, "Had you been doing your job you'd know that we've just been fired upon by a proton torpedo."

"Are you kidding me, what the hell, you all doing up there on the bridge? We don't have the shield capacity for that kind of impact, our shields are only meant for small asteroids and backing into loading docks."

"I know, I know." I reply. "And to make matters worse, Tony, the torpedo has breached the hull and we are now losing structural integrity."

"Really, where? What decks?"

"Decks one through five aft of the hangar bay have no power, and cargo bays twenty to twenty five are gone."

"Frack, this is bad man, really bad, and what do you want from me?"

"I want you to fix the problem Tony, a-sap."

"You do know I'm on strike right, this is your problem now Captain, you gotta fix it." He said matter of factly.

"Tony here's the thing, YOU'RE A FRIKKEN MAINTENANCE MAN SO YOU GOTTA DO IT AND THAT'S AN ORDER!" I say yelling into the mike. "Tony we are losing structural integrity and all your doing is standing around with your thumb up your ass playing CARD GAMES! This ship is as much your home as it is mine, if this breach doesn't get fixed right away we are going to implode. I for one don't want my ass to be considered part of the superstructure when it does got it, NOW FIX THE BREACH!"

"Alright, alright I'll fix it.

"Good."

"So what do you have in mind?"

'Wow, really, did he just say that? Unbelievable, is it just me or does my crew really can't think for themselves?' I thought incredusally.

I sigh in frustration and just shake my head. "Ok, Chief, erect a structural containment field around the breach, that should hold till we get to Orion Station. Once the containment field is up, purge the inside to get rid of the cosmic radiation. Once that's done go inside and save as much of the cargo as you can, I'm going on an away mission so the ship will be stationary giving you time to make the necessary repairs. Now get it done, you have your orders." And without hearing a protest from the chief of maintenance I turn off his channel.

I then leave Marvin to his machinations and head to my ready room to deal with the two junior crew men waiting for me. I get halfway across the bridge when the ship's science officer, L.T. Leon Fernandez stops me.

"Captain?"

"What is it Leon and make it fast?"

"I want to go on the away mission too."

"No, you're staying here on the Supernova."

"But Captain I have military training too and that's why I want to go. Also I think I would be an asset and not a hindrance."

"Oh, how so?" I eye Leon sceptically while crossing my arms.

"I'm the best tech guy you have on this ship and the only one on the bridge that's a fully trained field medic."

Surprised by this, I start thumbing through the bridge crew files on my command node to confirm what Leon had said was true. As I was doing this a thought occurred to me. 'I really gotta start paying more attention to my bridge crew's backgrounds, It seems to me I don't know a damn thing about them.'

Well, what Leon had said was true, he really did train as a field medic back in his brief military career. I smile and pat him on his shoulder. "That explains why I see you helping Dr Sune in the med labs all the time. Alright Lieutenant, go find Lee and help him sort through the crew's files and give him a hand bringing his weapons to the hanger bay, I'll see you down there shortly."

"Eye Captain." Said Leon Fernandez with a salute, then he sped off the bridge toward the turbo lift and within a few seconds he was gone.

Once again I make my way to my ready room and this time it's Cranky stopping me. I had a feeling he was going to stop me and I was right. Cranky grabs onto my bicep and pulls me close so only I can hear.

"I have military training too." He whispers into my ear.

"I know James but you've got to stay here." I whisper. I take a step back, pull off my command node and hold it out for him, he looks down at it grabs it and looks back at me with a devilish grin and says to me. "So where doing this again are we?" He pulls off his node and holds it out for me, I grab it fit it in my wrist mount and I say with my own sly grin "Yes we are…, Captain."

I've mentioned before that Cranky should be captain of the Supernova. Well as a matter of fact a lot of people in the galaxy think he is. Actually let me rephrase, they think he's me. You see we've switched I.D.'s before. It's because a lot of people have a hard time believing that at the age of forty, I'm a captain of a star ship. Cranky's old and to most people it makes sense that an elderly person is a captain and not only that Cranky has an air about him and he plays a captain really, really, well. Which is why he should be Captain and not me.

This time is no different we're switching command nodes to fool the enemy into thinking we are each other, I still have access to my captain's commands via Cranky's node which makes things easier on away missions. This all came about because I have restricted clearance on unscheduled stops. In order for me to partake in unscheduled away missions I need to have a military rank of commander which I don't and Cranky does. So we switch I.D.'s. every now and then, what of it. Besides he is too old for this kind of away mission anyway.

So thanks to the ship's science officer L.T. Leon Fernandez and his genius tech ability, he was able to hack into both command nodes and assign our D.N.A. to one another's nodes. It fools computers into thinking we are each other, I'm Commander James Crane when I get scand and Cranky is me, Captain Mott.

This little illegal ruse is so I can eventually get my military rank of commander. I need the combat experience to challenge the testing at the military academy. Luckily for me there's still a war going on between the new empire, the former federation, all of the I.R.F. And other pirates in the galaxy as well. Once I get the commanders rank added to my captaincy, I won't have to use Cranky's node to get clearance on unscheduled stops anymore. Then, I can pursue the rank of commodore, granting me two Strike cruisers in the near future to defend the Supernova from pirate attacks which have become a plague in the galaxy, and the worst by far are the I.R.F. that's the Interstellar, Response, Force. Again I'll get to them in a moment. First I need to explain some more about my captaincy.

I'm what's considered a merchant vessel captain not a merchant marine vessel captain the difference is the merchant marine are considered navy and right now I'm considered civilian and I need military contracts to keep this ship operational.

Nova-tech provides only so much contracts, the pay is alright, but with the rising cost of fuel and maintaining this ship I need to branch out and acquire those lucrative military contracts. To do this I need to obtain a commodores rank, then I become part of the Emperors merchant marine granting me two Orillian strike cruisers and one company of marine corps operatives from each ship, that's five hundred fully armed and armoured ground crew from each company, a thousand troops in total at my command. To obtain all of this I need a military rank of commander, luckily for me Cranky has the rank and the ground clearance I need for unscheduled dock access.

If the Supernova were a navy vessel we would have access to ground troops that the old fart named Cranky would be in charge of, however we're not we're just a civilian vessel so I gotta take with me what I already have, Lieutenant Commander Lee frikken Oswald. He's awesome in a firefight, but figgity as all getup the rest of the time. As for L.T. Leon Fernandez, well this will be his first combat type away mission, and totally unproven in a hostile environment. I hope Leon can keep a level head when shit goes sideways and knowing my luck it probably will.

Be that as it may, Cranky monitores my combat training through my captains node and pretends to be me. And when he has to respond to the enemy in a few minutes, the enemy will undoubtedly run a D.N.A. scan then they will see an old man and thinks he is me. I mean him, I mean me, ya, you get the idea. Cranky has been telling me for the past year that I have only one more combat away mission then I can challenge the testing at the military academy. Will I be able to get my commanders rank if I survive this mission I wonder? Only time will tell. So for the time being I have to use Cranky's node.

You are all probably wondering why I need combat training in the first place? Well like I said pirates have become a serious problem in the galaxy and they will stop at nothing to obtain their malevolent goals. Including boarding Civilian freighters, killing the crew and making off with the ship. Even now pirates blow a hole in the side of my ship with a potential hostile confrontation with them when i shuttle down to colonies surface. Which brings me back to the I.R.F. and in case you forgot that's the Interstellar, Response, Force.

And now for a little history lesson. Out past the Orion Nebula in the Orion Arm of our beloved Milky Way Galaxy, lies a planetary colony called Orilon. After twelve generations of human population living on this planet, which are the original bloodlines of the colonies founding by the way, the humans have developed traits due to enzymes in the planet's atmosphere and environment. These enzymatic traits have caused the orillian humans to grow taller, become smarter and much stronger than the average human living elsewhere in the galaxy.

Being so far from our solar system the orillian humans that governed the population on planet Orilon eventually thought they were being abandoned by the federation. Communication takes a long time to reach Orilon from Earth thanks to the Orion Nebula and the delay was worse this time.

With limited communication and unbenounced to the federation, the planet went dark for twenty six years, no word was getting in or out of Orilon, because of a massive ion storm in the Orion Nebula, yes the ion storm lasted that long. Then a militant uprising calling themselves the I.M.P. That's the Intergalactic, Military, Power, swept into the Federal Orilon Government and with lethal force systematically took over. The I.M.P, started to impose harsher laws on the civilian population. Martial law led to Irrational convictions. As the prisons became overcrowded, the I.M.P, governors of the planet saw that they had no choice, but to start youthaniseing the newly convicted civilians. The deaths, led to the planet wide revolt.

One man rose to power after his wife and children were taken by the I.M.P. Luckily He served in the F.A.F. That's the Federal Armed Forces. He rallied his fellow officers together and formed a successful siege on the capital city of his continent and got his family back. From this Rescue he staged a successful coup which spread his revolution around the planet and laid the foundations for his empire.

After he subjugated the I.M.P's leaders into his new regime, and changed F.A.F. to the P.I.M.P.S. That's the Planetary Intergalactic Magistrate Police Service.or pimps as I call them. And the Intergalactic Military Power is now the I.M.P.S.Or imps as i call them. And they are now the Intergalactic Magistrate Police Service and the heads of his new governing military judicial system. This one man then went on to rule the entire planet's civilian population. The people have sworn their allegiance to him, and declared him Emperor of Orilon.

Then he decided that the rest of the galaxy must surrender to his imperial rule too. So he set his civilian population to work and built his fleet of starships and formed the other militant wing of the I.M.P.S. They are the Cosmic Highway Intergalactic Magistrate Police Service. The C.H.I.M.P.S. or chimps as I call them.

Finally the ion storm abated and when communication was finally received on Planet Earth the federation's officials were shocked to see a growing fleet of cosmic war ships orbiting Orilon and one man declaring himself Emperor. His name is Efron Solace Octavian or the emperor of humanity as he calls himself.

Then the ion storm intensified once again and communication was halted once more. The federation fearing an invasion from Orilon quickly responded to this rebellious leader. In conjunction with the federal armed forces also known as the F.A.F. And knowing that Orilon humans are far superior even in combat, the federation in turn created twenty six legions of super soldiers to quell the rebellion and bring Orilon back into its fold. These legions are known throughout the galaxy as the Interstellar, Response, Force, or the I.R.F. as they are more commonly referred to.

The I.R.F. was the federations state of the art military force and fleet. The men and women who volunteered for the program from the F.A.F. underwent a rigorous bionic and cybernetic implantation process. The ones that survived the augmentation of their bodies went on to become a trooper in the Interstellar Response Force. This program was called the Valhallen Project and it had created twenty six I.R.F. Legions.

The I.R.F. Legions and its fleets were not prepared for the technological advancement of the orillian armed forces. Up until now energy weapons were only in sci-fi stories. Although the I.R.F. used state of the art weapons of the highest quality they were no match for the orillian energy weapons even the Orilon starships had energy weapons and they all but eliminated the I.R.F. fleet.

The emperor and his forces did not stop until the federation surrendered almost a year ago or so his imperial majesty says, and the only thing that has changed is that one man now tries to control the stars instead of the federation and the war marches on.

As for the I.R.F. They've all but disappeared into obscurity, leaving only speculation and rumors of their whereabouts. Which is not surprising because after the so called collapse of the federation all I.R.F. troops had to register under the new regime. A lot went rogue and turned to piracy and they are still waging war against the Emperor's forces every chance they get.

The I.R.F. have now become infamous and urban legends in their own right, now conspiracy theorists think they've never existed at all. What a load of crap, they do exist and they're bad really bad. I just hope that the pirates of Midas Eighty Eight are not the I.R.F.

All of a sudden I realised something, I look back across the bridge and holler out to my communications officer. "Hey Marvin, I seem to have forgotten something important." Marvin turned around in his chair and looks at me. "When I'm gone try to find as much information as you can on this Admiral Kruel, can you do that for me?"

"Yes Captain, I can do that for ya."

"Thanks Marv, and Cranky, you help Marvin as well, got it, you have your orders."

I finally walk inside my ready room which is sparsely furnished, and two junior bridge officers stand nervously in front of my desk.

I sit down in my plush chair tap the comms and lean back with my feet up on the desk.

"Hello Samantha." I say with a sly tone.

The female voice on the other end sounded a bit irate.

"It's about time John you know I don't like being put on standby."

"It's Captain, is that too much to ask to be called Captain?" I replied sitting up in my chair and leaning my elbows on the desk now.

"John the day I call you Captain is the day I get tortured by the I.R.F."

"I can arrange that you know." I said sarcastically

"Ha ha very funny just what the hell did you run into that flung me from my bed anyway?"

"I did not run into anything in fact something ran into us."

"What was it?" She asked in a curious tone.

"A proton torpedo." I reply.

"What! We don't have the shield capacity for that kind of impact our shields are only meant for small asteroids and backing into loading docks."

"I know, I know." I say rolling my eyes.

"Are there any injuries, deaths, how bad is the damage? She inquires with a hint of panic in her voice.

"You'll be happy to know there are no injuries or deaths and It's a good thing no one was scheduled for cargo inspection at the time of impact, because all the damage was centered on cargo bays twenty to twenty five, also decks one through five aft of the hangar bay has no power as well.

"Oh thank the stars there were no casualties." she said relieved. "So what are you doing about the decks with no power and the destroyed cargo bays?"

"I've managed to get Chief Florin to fix the problem, he and his crew are working on it right now as we speak."

"Wow, colour me impressed John, you've actually managed to get someone who's on strike to go back to work. How'd you manage to pull that off?"

"Despite what you may think Samantha, I do have a way with people."

"I know you do, you just yell at them to get what you want, just like my grandpa does."

"I don't yell, I reason with people and sometimes it gets a little loud."

"Is that what you call your yelling at the crew, reasoning?"

"That is what I call it. Now then, to the matter at hand." I say changing the subject. "I have two of your bridge crew in my ready room right now and they look like they are about wet themselves from fright. Just what do you do to make them so nervous all the time? See Samantha I'm not yelling I'm reasoning."

"Not yet anyway, and to answer your question John, I don't make them nervous you do."

I ignore the he said she said and direct the conversation off of me. "So tell me Commander why are these two junior bridge officers past their shift?"

There was a slight pause before she answered which raised my eyebrow in suspicion.

"I don't know why, John." she finally said "They know they aren't supposed to be I'll reprimand them when I go back on duty." who are they?

"You know who they are and I'll do it now. Have a good sleep Commander. Captain out."

I shut off the link to my ready room before she has a chance to protest and inquire about her two subordinates. I then turned my attention back to the two junior bridge officers standing frightfully in front of my desk.

"Ok, both of you know as well as I do she is full of B.S. right? I give the two subordinates a stern look pressing the issue, while leaning my elbow on my desk with an accusing finger pointing at them. They just stood there like a couple of frightened school children not saying a word. So I continued.

"Your commander knows damn well that she ordered you two to stay after your shift, am I right? Speak!" I order, maybe a little too sternly.

"Yes Captain." Replied the subordinate on my left. "Commander Samantha Crane ordered us to stay past our shift.

"I thought as much, I just wanted you to tell me the truth that's all. And don't worry I'm not going to reprimand you two for following your orders even if there's no point to it, all she has to do is ask me for my end day report which will fill her in on all the days activities when she goes on duty." I then look to the young man on my left. "What's your name son?" I ask.

"I'm Acting Sub Lieutenant Tyrel Johnson Junior Class, Sir." Said the young man puffing out his chest and saluting me.

I bring up Tyrel's file on my desktop computer, which is actually my desktop, and to my surprise he did one tour of duty in the colony war. "Your former I.R.F. I say in amazement."

"Yes sir." Replies the young man. "I survived my augmentation and went on to be a trooper in Zulu Company, of the Interstellar, Response, Force. Then Emperor Octavian forced his registry of all federation combatants. After I registered in the new regime I was given a commision on the Supernova"

"That's excellent, Acting Sub Lieutenant Johnson." I smile as I look to the other subordinate who is standing rigidly quiet. "And what's your name?"

"I'm Acting Sub Lieutenant Kenny Kubota Junior Class, Sir." He also puffed out his chest and saluted me before he continued. "I too survived my implantation process and I'm also from Zulu Company. Did you know that Zulu Company is the only company to have a one hundred percent augmentation survival rate?"

"I did not know that." I answer.

"Kenny Kubota continues. "Our company." he points his thumb at his companion. "Is the last company to be created by the former federation and by the time the scientists created Zulu company all research had been perfected with a zero percent mortality rate and no reported augmentation psychosis. For a million creds you too can be augmented you know Sir?"

"Why would I want that it sounds awful. At any rate, how would you two like to be put on security detail, and be under the direct command of Lieutenant Commander Lee Oswald? I will also strip away the Junior classification, what do you say?

The two junior officers look to one another and back at me in surprise. Clearly they were not expecting promotions after I just gave them heck for being past their shift.

"Think about it and when we get to Orion Station I'll make your promotions official. Until then I'm conscripting you two under my command and you're coming with me on this away mission.

"Uh Captain?" Asks Tyrel Johnson. "We are exhausted and we need rest to be effective in our combat rolls.

Then Kenny pipes in. "Even with our enhancements we still need rest Captain?"

"Don't worry about that, L.T. Leon Fernandez has something you can take that will remove your fatigue for this mission. We have no time to lose go get your gear and meet me at my quarters in ten minutes. You have your orders, dismissed.

"Yes Sir." They saluted and ducked out of my ready room in seconds.

Five minutes later I'm gathering up the gear I need for this away mission in my quarters when I notice something tucked away in the back of my closet. This container is a type of suit bag, I pull the cumbersome container out of the closet and place it on my bed. The container had my name on it which was strange because I have no recollection of owning this type of clothing apparatus. I open the container and a black silky garment reveals itself under the light of my quarters, on top of the article of clothing is a note addressed to me, which I read.

Captain, I have created a wonderful piece of clothing that you may get the chance to use soon. What you are looking at if you are reading this, is called a body glove or carapace, it is made of nanotech micro fibers that when worn molds around you like an outer skin or "carapace". The technology in the microfibers produce microscopic needles that enter your skin at certain points to affect your performance in a positive way, these points are based on acupuncture theories. However the body glove only works when combined with your environmental hard suit, which I took the liberty of making some alterations: One, your hard suit now has a direct link with the carapace giving you superior mobility, it will feel like you are not wearing a hard suit at all.

Two, the backpack of your hard suit is not only your life support systems, it now also produces a performance enhancing placebo, through the microscopic needles of the body glove. You are now a supersoldier like the I.R.F. without the painful augmentation operation that they go through. Pretty cool huh.

P.S. Let me know how well the carapace works so I can either make some more for the crew or not.

Your loyal science officer L.T. Leon Fernandez.

I smile a very wide grin and strip down to my skivvies in mere seconds, I slip into the body glove and a millisecond later I yelp in pain. It felt like I had just been struck by lightning as millions of microscopic needles enter my body all at once. "What the hell, Leon!" I cry out. And just like that a nanosecond later the pain is gone. I wipe the tears from my eyes, ya thats right tears, that was the most searing pain I've ever felt ok, even though it was for only a microsecond, still that sucked. And to think I've got to go through that every time I put on the body glove. Bloody hell!

In the moment I've collected my composure, I open the locker that contains my hard suit. I start putting it on and that's when I notice strange metallic circles on my body glove light up, once the pieces of the hard suit where over the lit up circles I felt presser like something just got connected. A moment later I'm sealed in my hard suit, I thumb the toggle for the life support system and as my suit powers up, a change happens.

To describe this change I would say this. A kaleidoscope of sensory perception hit me like a tidal wave of emotions all at once, and when it stopped I was aware of everything around me, I saw things in a new light, I felt things too; like the floor underneath me, the walls around me, the people on this ship, the two men waiting for me outside my door to my quarters. I felt for the first time like I was alive and I knew without a doubt that my science officer gave me a special gift.

Leon wasn't exaggerating when he wrote in his note that it would feel like I'm not wearing my environmental hard suit. Hard suits at the best of times are very cumbersome, motorized actuators help with your mobility while in gravity but it still requires a lot of conditioning to build up the strength you need to move in a hard suit. However they do work best in zero gravity. But this, this is something altogether better, I don't have to lug myself around in a clumsy suit of armour and walk like an angry robot from those black and white sci-fi movies of the ancient past. I love those black and white sci-fi movies by the way. What a moment in time, just on the cusp of space travel and those wonderful old movies helped launch science and technology to new heights. People had dreams of making space flight a reality back then, I'm glad they did.

I hit the door button and swoosh! it slides open. My two conscripted junior officers and former I.R.F. Troopers Kenny Kubota and Tyrel Johnson stood before me.

"Captain." They say together and both salute me like they've been rehearsing this motion for months.

"Alright you guys that's enough, I love your discipline and all but let's make one thing clear, drop the Captain and saluting me right now. For this op you will refer to me as Commander or Commander Crane is that clear?"

"Yes Sir." They say together.

Wow it was like they were hard wired together or something, I just may have to call them bot one and bot two from now on.

"Uh, Captain I have a question?" Asks Kenny Kubota while raising his hand up like an intimidated school kid.

Now I sternly point at him. "Didn't I just say not to call me captain, for the love of the cosmos, pull it together man, and put your hand down, were not in school you look foolish. Now what is it Kenny? Walk and talk."

We then head for the turbo lift that will take us down to the lobby of the tramway and our ride to the hangar bay.

"Well sir, I've been wondering why do we need to call you Commander or Commander Crane?"

"Because, I want the enemy to think I'm Commander Crane, and he's playing me. Besides Cranky's too old for surface operations, so I do it. Only a ranking officer with military citations is allowed clearance on unscheduled docks. I don't have any military citations, so I therefore assume the role of one Commander James Crane. Now I'll say this one last time call me Commander or Commander Crane got it?"

Then Tyrel piped up. "How about we just call you sir."

"That works too." I reply as I hit the button for the turbo lift doors to open.

As soon as the doors close on the turbo lift the elegant sounds of Max Weight and The Moose Whistles accost our ears, typical, elevator music for our elevator.

"When did that get installed?" I wonder out loud.

Once again our nubian friend Tyrel pipes up. "Studies have shown that elevator music does have a calming effect on people while riding in one, it lowers stress levels in people who don't like small spaces especially when descending."

I don't know which was worse, the elevator music or hearing about how elevator music makes you feel while riding in one. I do know this for sure, I was more stressed out when the doors finally opened to the tram lobby, than when I got in the turbo lift. What the hell!"

You know how I've mentioned before that the Supernova is fifteen kilometers long and two point five kilometers wide? Well, if we had to walk the length and breadth of the ship it would take all day and nothing would get done. So maglevs where installed to take the crew around the ship within minutes.

The lower deck tram as we call them, was waiting for us, sometimes it's not there, so we have to wait a few minutes but not this time. I hit the start button and a computerized voice blurts out its programed nuance. "Destination please?"

"Hangar bay" I order.

"Thank you Captain Mott, and have a pleasant day." seconds later we accelerate toward the hangar bay. I touch Cranky's command node and the computer blurts out again. "Thank you Commander Crane and have a pleasant day."

"That's better, see guys even the Supernova can follow orders."

We arrive in the hangar bay and the hustle and bustle of ordered commotion fills our view. It's always a wonder to behold the enormity of it all. One kilometer high rises the ceiling onward and upward past gangways and craneways, wires, cables and finally the arc lights. A technology that lights the hangar like day. This technology is called arcanology something that I can't begin to fathom. This is some of our tech from Orilon that the Emperor made us instal while we were at dock orbiting Earth. The people that make it are known as Arcanologists, and they are almost always from Orilon. Their order is very secretive and quite religious in nature with the head of the order on the Supernova known as an arcanist, and the lower ranking members are known as arcalytes.

Once a month I have a meeting with all the heads of my departments, heads of state I call them and when I meet with the head arcanologist. Arcanist Madam Millenius is her name, I always have to dress in formal attire because the woman is always formal herself and it's very odd, but that's a story for another time.

Above the arc lights rising for another kilometer are the cargo bays and above that are decks going up for another kilometer, this is also where Leon spends most of his off duty time. His favorite place being a science officer and all, are the science and medical labs and also the cryo engineering center. Actually it's the cryo engineering center that Leon has taken over having no engineers on board for our departments Leon decided to run the cryo engineering center which happen to be beside the science and medical labs labs. I think he has a thing for Dr. Mayling Sune the head of medical here on the Supernova whatever the case he spends his off duty time in the cryo center.

I could not see to the far end of the hangar bay because of all the organized chaos going on, still the far wall would barley be visible anyway being two point five kilometers away. We traverse down the tram platform stairwell to the hangar bay floor and another ride was waiting for me. A little four passenger yellow maintenance cart complete with an orange beacon was to the right of the stairs. "I'll drive." I told bot one and bot two. We climb in, I fire it up and whisk us away to the shuttle platform. I knew the cart was going to be there waiting for me because today was the day, I, Captain Mott was making an appearance in the hangar bay and that meant no slacking off. Although that's not the case my chief executive officer of the ships logistics center a man in his mid fifties named Clancy Grover runs the hangar bay like a well oiled machine. He new I was on my way to the hangar bay and made sure the maintenance cart was waiting for me.

As we make our way to launch control where my Falcon Class shuttle awaited our arrival, I turn my head and yell out over the cacophony of machinery milling about the hangar. "I hope Oswald and Fernandez found more volunteers for the away mission?"

"What Sir?" Yells Tyrel back at me.

"Nothing, we'll be at the shuttle in about three minutes!"

Both my companions just nod.

A few minutes later we arrive at the launch pad and sitting three meters above us is the Falcon Class shuttle that will take us to Midas Eighty Eight. The interesting thing about the Falcon Class shuttle is that it also has a military application that changes its classification from the Falcon Class shuttle to the Firehawk Gunship without making any changes to the bird of prey body style, all you do is add the necessary armaments and voila it goes from a shuttle to a starfighter in under an hour. I think that's pretty frikken cool. Unfortunately my Falcon is only a shuttle.

We get to the top of the launch pad after climbing a set of stairs and I expected to see enough people to fill the shuttle to capacity. What I saw instead was in truth a disappointment to me. All I saw was Leon Fernandez helping Lee Oswald lug one of Lee's weapon crates into the shuttle and our pilot Jaxina Bernardino leaning against the fuel container doing something on a tablet and vaping nicotine while our shuttle was fueling.

'I wish Jaxina had a Class A starship pilot rating, she's a much better helmsman than Don Watts is. Don't get me wrong Don is an excellent helmsman, don't let him hear that though, it will go straight to his head and believe me I want this kid thinking he can do better. Be that as it may Jaxina is a much better pilot.

Jaxina looks up at us as we cross the deck to the shuttle and she trots over to us. She comments to me once she's in ear shot and points to bots one and two.

"Since when do you go on away missions with bodyguards?"

"Ha,ha, funny lady, they aren't bodyguards but I do need all the help I can get on this away mission. I asked Lee to sift through the crews files hoping to find crew members with military backgrounds, and you know, I was expecting to see more people here. I guess I'm not that lucky. So let me introduce you to these two gentlemen. Jaxina this is Acting Sub Lieutenant Tyrel Johnson and Acting Sub Lieutenant Kenny Kubota both junior class and both are former I.R.F. Troopers. Guys this is Sub Lieutenant Jaxina Bernardino junior class, our pilot."

"It's a pleasure." Said Tyrel shaking her hand.

"Likewise." Said Kenny Kubota also shaking her hand.

"You two are former I.R.F. eh, Oswald is going to love you, he's also former I.R.F. You know?" She said pulling back her hand and slipping on a pair of old school aviators.

Both Kenny and Tyrel look at me surprised. "Why do you think I was excited when I found out that you were former I.R.F. and asked if you wanted to be under the command of Lee Oswald."

"What company is he from?" Asked Acting Sub Lieutenant Kenny Kubota, junior class of the star freighter known as the Supernova.

"That's something you're going to have to ask the Lieutenant Commander." I reply.

"Alright you ladies let's get this show on the road!" I order and wink at Jaxina as well.

Jaxina just smiles and shakes her head as we all embark the Falcon.

It turns out that the only crew members with military backgrounds on the Supernova are as follows: Commander James Crane and he's too old to come, his grand daughter Commander Samantha

Crane Junior Class, I know what you're thinking too why am I not bringing Samantha, well she has to be here to run the night crew.

Next is communications officer Lieutenant Marvin Lewinsky, military classification only, no actual combat experience only simulation, besides he has to stay on the ship as well and monitor the communications.

Science officer Lieutenant Leon Fernandez, he also has no combat experience either, but he has a field medic classification and he already has proven he can patch people up because he sometimes helps Dr. Mayling Sune in the med labs and that's why he's coming.

Lieutenant Commander Lee Oswald of course, he always goes on away missions with me, ever since he was commissioned on the Supernova, the two former I.R.F. troopers and Acting Sub Lieutenants Tyrel Johnson and Kenny Kubota both junior class, I don't need to go into detail about these guys.

Jaxina Bernardino my personal pilot, this is the only Falcon Class shuttle on the Supernova and it's mine all the other shuttles on the ship are bulky and slow and used for transferring cargo from the Supernova to logistics centers and vice versa. Like I said Jaxina is a much better pilot than Don Watts is, because her pilot rating is all military, she's actually a starfighter pilot that has seen combat in the war before I commissioned her as my personal pilot here on the Supernova.

And last but not least is myself, I have a pilot rating too and I know I can fly the Falcon as well as Jaxina can, but why should I, I'm now the Captain of the Supernova. I just spent the last twenty years working my way up through the ranks piloting everything on this ship and the ship itself, I don't need to prove that I have what it takes to fly and I also proved time and time again that I'm a good soldier.

I can't believe that out of the four thousand crew members on board the Supernova all I get are eight people with military backgrounds, come on really.

We launch from the Supernova and I quickly use Commander James Crane's command node to give us encrypted military clearance on Midas Eighty Eight. As Jaxina was piloting the falcon, new information was passing through her flight consul that will let us pass undetected to the surface of the colony. Not long after we launch we arrive at the asteroid colony. Suddenly the encryption codes were working over time as we shuttle down through the obscure technology of the biodome to the landing pad of the logistics center of Midas Eighty Eight. Clearly someone had put up security measures to keep us out. I hope Cranky's codes will work?

F.Y.I. we don't call major cargo ports, ports anymore they are now called spaceports and they are for civilians and their personal items, cargo ports are now called logistics centers.

Once the shuttle was safely on the landing pad and powering down I order all personnel within the shuttle to gather up their gear. I roll my eyes after we all get a walk through on the finer points of weapon use from Lieutenant Commander Lee Oswald. He always does this, I think it's part of his psychosis from his I.R.F. implants. Once Lee was done we all disembarked from the falcon leaving Jaxina to her machinations.

Normally a logistics center of this size would be very busy, however the silence of the place gave me a bad feeling in my gut.

"Lee do you get the feeling we are being watched?" I whisper.

"I get that feeling all the time." he whispers back

'Great, he's as paranoid as Marvin Lewinsky is.' I thought to myself while pulling my blaster gun from its holster.

I let Lee take point and he guided us through the logistics center single file. We took cover here and there behind cargo containers all the while scanning for signs of life. I couldn't help but notice how odd it was that the people who worked here seemed to just up and leave. Forklifts still had crates on them, gantry cranes still had containers attached, it was like work had not yet ended and that unnerved me.

We wound our way through the docking district until we got close to an office complex.

"That's the administration of the logistics center." I whisper.

Lee held up his fist in the universal sign to hold and take cover. We did so behind a container and the Lieutenant Commander turns to me and whispers. "We are getting close to the civilian district of the colony." And he points past the office complex to more buildings in the distance, then he continues. "I suggest we take our route through the offices who knows we might find intel on what has happened down here, what do you think?"

"Agreed, lead the way." I whisper. I do not get upset at Lee for the casual way he talks and for not calling me Commander or sir, he never does when we are on away missions, this is what he was born to do so I let him do his job. I touch Commander Crane's command node and the H.U.D. in my hardsuits helmet displayed the comms. Leon, Tyrel and Kenny's name were displayed up to my left along with their life signs, I look at their names and now I can communicate with the rest of my team, as you already know I was in communication with Lee and he was the one issuing orders to the rest of the team, his name was also up to the left in my H.U.D.

"Stay alert we are going to make for the offices and keep an eye out for marksmen in the windows luckily no one will be there but you never know." I whisper to the team. And in response I get a roger that from my fire team.

I look over to Leon kneeling beside me and I notice his weapon of choice, it was a marksman rifle. I quickly thumb the command node on my wrist and bring up Leon's file again, as I was scrolling through it Lee decided to take Kenny with him to cover another area of approach.

"Leon I noticed your choice in weapon and did some more research on your file too, top of your class in marksmanship think you can recon the building for us?"

"Ya sure." He replies.

"Lee hold up, let Leon recon the building before we move." I whisper to my second in command.

"Good thing I'm in cover." Lee whispers back.

Leon moves around me to get to the edge of the container we were taking cover behind and braces himself while kneeling in a marksman pose.

"Sir I spot movement on the top floor of the office." Whispers the science officer

"Can you make out more details?" I whisper. In response to my inquiry Leon whispers back to me.

"Yup, the man is dressed in an official uniform."

"Ok move Leon, I need a look." I demand in a harsh whisper as I holster my blaster gun.

The cool thing about my command hardsuits helmet eye control heads up display or H.U.D. as we call it. I look therefore I get and I zoom in on the top floor of the office complex.

"Ok Leon where is he?" I whisper out my command.

"Last window on the left." Came the whispered reply

"Ok got him, It's the C.E.O of the logistics center." I say to the team. More coolness from my H.U.D. It's identity software ran a scan of the C.E.O.'s holobadge and his work file appeared scrolling before my eyes. His name was Berry Michael Yevon Lecar.

"Wow really Berry.M.Y.Lecar." I heard snickers from my men just then.

"Calm down guys it's not that funny."

"Commander it's your call on how you want to play this?" Said Lieutenant Commander Lee Oswald still chuckling.

I saw Lee scanning to the North East of the office complex and noticed what he was looking at, it was an airlock that lead somewhere to the buildings beyond the logistics center. I also notice that off to my right of the office complex was a fortified wall that ran the length of the biodome out to the east toward the spaceport and customs. This was indeed a stronghold with high level security.and that airlock that Lee was aiming at was a concern. No small wonder that this place would be fortified with this much gold at stake. I'm starting to think this was a mistake coming here. I can't let the others know my apprehension.

I notice the Lieutenant Commander was hiding in the shadows of another container with Kenny Kubota watching his back.

'Good the team is bonding as well.' I thought.

Lieutenant Commander Lee Oswald is former I.R.F. And for some reason other augmented people like former I.R.F. troopers seem to be naturally drawn to him and vice versa, I have seen this before it doesn't always happen mind you, but in this case it's Kenny that's drawn to Lee and the Lieutenant Commander's decision to bring Kenny with him to watch his back was not a random choice either it was a calculated decision, and Acting Sub Lieutenant junior class and former I.R.F. Trooper Kenny Kubota, will stop at nothing to protect Lee Oswald.

I turn to Leon Fernandez, who was beside me, and I ask him.

"Can you encrypt a message for me over the the general comms, so that only the C.E.O. Will get it I wanna talk to this guy?"

"I think so, it will take a minute or two, because this is more of Marvin's expertise than mine but I think I can do it."

"Good." and I notice Leon scanning the area looking for something. "Leon what are you looking for?" I ask in a whisper.

Leon whispers back as he was still scanning the area. "I'm looking for the R.C.M.P."

"The R.C.M.P. what for they haven't existed for thousands of years. I knew you were highly educated Leon but I didn't know you were a history buff as well. Did you know I spent my vacation traveling around the North American continent and I discovered a law enforcement museum that had somehow managed to escape destruction from the emperor's attack. The museum dedicated a whole wing to the R.C.M.P. that's the Royal Canadian Mounted Police. It was quite fascinating, did you know they were the oldest police force in North America?"

Leon just looks at me dumbfounded. "Commander, what the hell are you talking about?" He finally says to me.

"You know the R.C.M.P. the royal canadian mounted police?" I reply.

"Why would I be looking for an old police force that has not existed for thousands of years?" Conjectured Leon.

"Because you're looking for the R.C.M.P. that's why." I retort.

"Yes Commander I am looking for the R.C.M.P. The radar controlled maintenance panel you laser brain."

"Oh, well why didn't you say so in the first place?" I say in a raised voice.

"I thought you knew what I was talking about." He said in the same tone.

"Leon, why would I know what the hell you're talking about, half the time its science related and a complete mystery to me."

He gave me a rude gesture and I gave one back then Leon spotted what he was looking for and ushered me to follow him, I did the same for Tyrel to follow as well, and the former I.R.F. Trooper did so without hesitation, all the while covering our backs.

We retrace our steps back the way we had come until we came upon a power junction.

A large yellow power generator vibrated and hummed as did the cables that linked it to a tall communications pilon. It was the communications pilon that Leon Fernandez sot out. He pointed to a yellow box with a red holographic face and with a sheepish grin he commented.

"This sir is the R.C.M.P. you know the radar controlled maintenance panel I was looking for."

I heard the sarcasm in his voice and I got a little bit annoyed.

"You know what?" I reply looking at Leon with a little disdain in my eye and jabbing a finger in his chest. "From now on, no more acronyms unless I know the acronym or come up with them myself, got it? Now hurry up!"

"Yes sir." He said a little deflated. And then my science officer from the bridge of the Supernova pulls from his med pack a multi-tool with wires and diodes coming out of it like it had some kind of crazy hair-do. Then Leon attaches some of the wires to my hard suit's back pack as well as the R.C.M.P. Box and comments.

"Alright this is going to take a little longer than I originally thought, it's got security measures in place, I must break down the fire walls first before I have full access to the innards of the panel, so bear with me ok."

"Leon we don't need your device to access this panel." I say with impatience. "I have all the access we need right here." I pull my blaster gun from its holster take aim and fire.

"No!" Yells Leon.

Within a nano second later the radar controlled maintenance panel explodes in a shower of sparks and after the smoke clears I see the holographic face is gone and the electronics inside can be clearly seen.

"See we're in." I say pointing my thumb at the exposed innards to express this fact.

"You knucklehead, you've just alerted the enemy to our location." Said a frantic Lieutenant Fernandez. "If you weren't my commanding officer I'd shoot you myself."

"Luckily for me I am your commanding officer, now patch me in to Mr. Lecar, and make it snappy Lieutenant!"

I just wanna go on record here, that while I may give my bridge crew a hard time about being incompetent, Lieutenant Leon Fernandez is the only crew member of mine that talks to me the way I talk to the rest of the bridge crew, ya I know this is his first away mission with potential hostilities and it won't be his last either he's handling himself somewhat professionally. That being said Leon is probably the only member of the bridge crew besides me of course that is not incompetent. Yes I screw up sometimes I'm only human after all and I know it frustrates the hell out of him when I do screw up. I also do it on purpose too. You see, I hate feeling like I'm incompetent so I complicate things for him just to aggravate him.

"Ok Commander, you're patched in and because of that amusing show of gunmanship you just did I don't know if you are encrypted or not."

"Berry Lecar this is Commander James Crane of the starfreighter Supernova can you hear me?"

At first I get static then a staticy voice comes over the comms in my hard suite's helmet.

"Comm….Ander, this… Berry… Car."

I look at Leon and ask. "Can you clean this up he's not coming in clear?"

"I'll try, the R.C.M.P. has taken a lot of damage and he gives me a dirty look." Leon then attaches more wires from his multi-tool to some of the exposed electronic components this time. "Ok try it now." He said a moment later.

"Berry Lecar can you hear me?" I ask again.

"Yes loud and clear Commander, thank the stars you're here."

I give Leon a thumbs up.

"Listen Commander something happened a minute ago that alerted the pirates to the docks."

Right then I knew Leon was listening to the conversation because he gave me a stern look.

"We need to leave, these pirates don't take prisoners, where are you?" I could hear the fear and urgency in Mr. Lecar's voice as I replied back.

"I'm over at the comms pilon by dock two can you get over hear?"

"Yes commander I'm on my way, see you in a minute or two." And then the comms went dead.

"Lee the CEO is coming out of the admin offices to rendezvous with us, I want you and Kenny to provide cover and protect him while you make your way over to where Leon and I are waiting. We are at the comms pilon, I'll use my locator beacon so you can track us down. Stay alert we have hostiles inbound."

"Roger that Commander see you shortly." Replied Lieutenant Commander Lee Oswald.

"Jaxina come in, can you hear me?" I demand to the shuttle pilot

"Yes Commander I can hear you what do you need?" Asks the female voice in my helmet.

"Get the shuttle ready for e-vac we're heading back to the Supernova as soon as we get there." I demand to her again.

"Eye, eye, Commander, Jaxina out."

A moment later I see Lieutenant Commander Lee Oswald leading his ward at a fast pace with Acting Sub Lieutenant Kenny Kaboata Junior Class in tow. The three of them made for the communications pilon where Lieutenant Leon Fernandez, Acting Sub Lieutenant Tyrel Johnson Junior Class and myself stood waiting. Once they got close to us I noticed Berry Lecar had a blaster gun in his hand, it was the same as mine, a federation issue P4 Ion shot blaster gun a truly remarkable side arm. I thought nothing of it at first and we fell in line and continued the brisk pace that Lee Oswald maintained, and we headed for the shuttle craft that would take us safely back to the Supernova.

I decided to introduce the rest of us.

"Berry Lecar, I'm Commander James Crane." I point to Leon. "This is Lieutenant Leon Fernandez and Acting Sub Lieutenant Tyrel Johnson security detail. I take it that you have been introduced to Lee and Kenny already?"

"Yes Commander they were waiting for me when I left the admin offices." He said through puffs of breath while jogging toward our waiting pilot.

"I know Mr Lecar I ordered them to wait for you. Now then this is what we are going to do, we are going to shuttle you back to the Supernova, once there you are going to tell me everything that happened and then we are going to inform the authorities so that a proper plan can be put in place to rescue the colonists, assuming they are still alive."

"They are Commander and the majority of the colonists are being held in the mine I think. I hid in one of the engine housings of the tall gantry crane one of the ones used to offload and load the conveyance shuttles known as trucks." He points to a tall crane with its boom in the upright position "It's down for maintenance." He continues. "That's how I managed to stay hidden from the up rising I was Inspecting the engine at the time. It just happened so fast we are not prepared for this kind of situation. What are we going to do?"

"Calm down Mr Lecar, we will figure this out and come up with a good plan to rescue the remaining colonists. First things first getting you over to the Supernova safley." I say in my most calming and reassuring voice.

And this was when everything went to hell in a handbasket real fast. I noticed Kenny Kubota trailing behind us fiddling with his wrist mounted communicator node. Which is much like my command node but without the command functions. He kept holding it up every so often like he was scanning something and he kept doing this until we arrived at the bottom of the shuttle pad. I noticed Jaxina sitting at the top of the stairs vaping nicotine and smiling as we all clamoured around the bottom of the launch pad near the stairs. And through puffs of vapor she comments "The Falcon is ready for e-vac sir."

"Excellent Sub Lieutenant." I reply formally. I was just about to start climbing the stairs to get to the top of the launch pad when Kenny Kubota sunters up to me with a look of concern on his face.

"We have a problem sir." He finally says to me.

"What's the problem Kenny?" I ask informally while turning around to face him.

Why Kenny Kubota removed his hardsuit's helmet in the first place I will never know, but the acting sub lieutenant junior class of the Starfreighter known as the Supernova did not get the chance to tell me what he was so concerned about because his face exploded in a deluge of brain matter, skull fragments and chunks of eyeballs all over my hardsuits helmet, some visera landed on the stairs leading up to the top of the shuttle pad as well.

"Oh my god he just killed kenny, you bastard I will kill you!" Screamed Tyrel Johnson hysterically. While drawing a bead on Berry Lecar with his assault rifle. A high quality prototype.

The I.R.F. A.R. 100. Assault Rifle.

Had Tyrel pulled the trigger, a 100mil round would have shredded Berry Lecar into pieces because the other thirty nine rounds would follow and a second later the man would be dead and game over for Berrey Lecar. You see the I.R.F. A.R. 100. Assault rifle holds one forty round magazine and fires forty rounds a second while in full auto mode, the ark technology that powers the weapon makes them have an insane rate of fire, no normal human can use it. The man holding said weapon however, is a fully augmented human and a former I.R.F. Trooper, powered up in an I.R.F. Bio reactive, military grade hard suit, is truly capable of using the assault rifle with ease. This man like all I.R.F. troopers can swap out a clip and change a new one in a second as well. I've seen Lieutenant Commander Lee Oswald do it and I know for a fact that Acting Sub Lieutenant Tyrel Johnson Junior Class can do it too. Unfortunately, he stayed his hand, as did the rest of the team when they aimed their weapons at Kenny's killer.

I wiped my visor free of the viscera that had smeared across it, I heard Jaxina vomiting from the top of the stairs and I almost did the same as a reflex.

"Oh my God!" She cried out, in between coughing and vomiting. "Why would you do that he was a good kid!"

Once I was able to see again I noticed we were all at a standoff, Berry Lecar was aiming his blaster gun at me and my crew were aiming their weapons at him. I never got the chance to draw my blaster gun because of all the gore that I was wiping off my helmet.

"Drop your weapons now or your commander is dead!" Demanded Berry Lecar forcibly.

"No, you drop your weapon!" Ordered Lieutenant Commander Lee Oswald. "We have you outgunned and outnumbered!"

"I don't think so, drop your weapons now because I have you all surrounded. Men!"

At that moment I knew we had just been played.

"Admiral Victor Kruel I presume?" I ask, still wiping viscera off my helmet.

"Very good Commander, now tell your people to drop their weapons."

All of a sudden we were surrounded by the Admiral's men and they were heavily armed and armoured. At this point a gun fight would be hopeless because we were also horribly outnumbered. I estimated the Admiral's force to be around fifteen men and they all had their weapons trained on us.I looked around at my crew members and motioned for them to drop their weapons. It's a good thing my crew can follow orders at times like this. As I was staring down the barrel of the Admiral's blaster gun, I breathed a sigh of relief when I heard the clatter of weapons hitting the ground.

"You didn't have to kill my crew member." I say clenching my fists in frustration and anger. "He was just a kid and I was going to be giving him a promotion."

"He was former I.R.F. just like the other two over there." Admiral Victor Kruel points to Lee Oswald and Tyrel Johnson, then he continues. "Your crew man would have had a melt down sooner or later and done something horrible it was just a matter of time.

Look at it as me doing you a favor Commander because I have prevented a tragedy."

"No Admiral you're wrong he was from Zulu Company they have a zero percent mortality rate, they don't suffer from any psychosis like the other legions do, so no tragedy would have befallen us."

"Really." The Admiral says in a curious tone looking down all of a sudden. Then Admiral Kruel kneels down by Kenny's corps and plucks something out of the bloody mess that was the dead man's head. I won't know the significance of what the Admiral took off Kenny's corps until a few months later from now.

"You know Admiral the only tragedy that I see here is the one you have made, not only were you sworn to protect the people of this mining colony you also have now commited murder in the name of piracy. And for what the gold, I don't think so, none of this makes any sense Admiral why are you doing this?"

"Well, well, Commander I'm actually truly impressed that you know about the murders. Yes I murdered Dr Roger Midal and the emissary from Orilon, this is war after all Commander. You see, Dr Midal was a traitor to the federation he was selling us out to this false Emperor, whom now claims the galaxy for all humanity. You are right Commander, I did swear an oath, I swore that I would protect the people of the Federation and I would also fight in the name of the Federation and I still do. When the emissary arrived from Orilon with legislation claiming that this was no longer a federation colony, I knew that it was Dr Midal that had betrayed the federation and when the majority of the people on this damn colony registered under the new regime, they became traitors too. That's why I had to take action and reclaim Midas Eighty Eight in the name of the Federation. Then you showed up and ruined everything. What you see surrounding you and your crew right now are the loyal soldiers of the Federation. When we took action, I killed Dr Midal and the emissary from Orilon and my men you see here rounded up the colonists and locked them in the mine. It was easier than I thought it was going to be hardly anyone put up a fuss. Oh well what's done is done I suppose. See Commander, now you know why I did what I had to do. We were being betrayed."

"You won't get away with this Admiral." I say in frustration.

"I already have Commander and who knows maybe I'll see you around sometime. Oh, and by the way thanks for getting the shuttle ready for e-vac you've really saved me the hassle. So know I must bid you a fond farewell."

And just like that the Admiral and his men picked up our discarded weapons, climbed the stairs to the top of the shuttle pad and a moment later the shuttle was lifting off and heading toward the obscure technology of the biodome.

PART TWO

THE SNAKE HAS NOTHING TO DO WITH THE BIRDS AND THE BEES

WE ALL WATCHED THE SHUTTLE disappear beyond the obscurity of the biodome technology, giving me unwanted momentary feelings of hopelessness and abandonment which was quickly replaced by feelings of frustration and anger with thoughts of retribution and revenge.

"What do we do now Captain?" Asks Lee Oswald turning to me with anger in his eyes and pointing to the sky. "That asshole just killed one of our own and stole our ride."

"I know Lee, now calm down, I will figure this out and get the shuttle back. Cranky can you still hear me?"

"Yes I can John and I guess we are calling you Captain now, don't worry the Falcon can't hear us, Sub Lieutenant Lewinsky is on top of things here on the Supernova."

"Well then, I guess we are going back to proper command." I shot Lee a contemptuous look for his laps in protocall and the man looked away from me embarrassed by his poor judgement and for letting his frustration get the better of him. "Oh and good work Marvin."

"Skipper I have to say that was a dumb thing shooting the R.C.M.P. Like that." Replies my first officer. "You scrambled the communications for a few nanoseconds, If you'd just waited for Lieutenant Fernandez to break down the fire walls with his multitool then Sub Lieutenant Lewinsky wouldn't have needed to defuse the electrical fire from the Supernova and potentially giving our location away. Then you would have been encrypted."

"Marvin has his uses too, I needed to see if he was paying attention to what was going on down here and not paying attention to deep space signals looking for alien messages and, besides it didn't matter, Admiral Kruel was alerted the moment we passed through the bio dome."

"Hey that's not fair Captain, I pay attention, most of the time."

"Zip it Lewinsky can't you hear the Captain and the First Officer are talking?" Ordered Lieutenant Commander Lee Oswald.

"You can it too Oswald!" Chastises Cranky. "Sub Lieutenant Marvin Lewinsky is a good bridge officer." Then Cranky returns talking with me again. "You think that's when the Admiral knew that someone had landed?"

"I do Commander." I answer.

I heard Marvin in the background mutter something like an insult toward Lieutenant Commander Lee Oswald and then complain about not going on away missions. Then Commander James Crane First Officer of the starfreighter known as the Supernova lived up to his nickname.

"Sub Lieutenant Lewinsky, we just lost a crew member, you know damn well your place is here on the bridge attending the communications now stop pouting and do your job!"

Then Marvin Lewinsky shouts back.

"But Commander, I've got combat experience too!"

I get in the act now. "Combat experience, like what, the combat simulators on the ship? Ha ha very funny Lewinsky, now put me on screen!" I soon see the inside of the bridge on the Supernova. And I can see Cranky and Marvin now, in my helmete's H.U.D. The first officer wasn't done his chastising of Marvin yet.

"Lieutenant Lewinsky, your military experience has always been in cosmic warfleet battles. Not ground combat and in your inexperience capacity, you will end up like Acting Sub Lieutenant Kenny Kubota Junior Class. Now be a good lad, turn around and pay attention to your monitor!"

"Yes Sir." As Marvin Lewinsky says this, I can see him hang his head slightly, and slowly turn his chair around. Then Cranky walks into my ready room and turns his attention back to me and tries to empathise with my situation and a moment later he says to me in a calming voice "How are you holding up Captain?"

I use the command node on my wrist to have a private conversation with my first officer and block out the rest of my crew, then I reply back to Cranky's inquiry.

"I've had better days that's for sure, shit I've just lost a crew member that's never happened before, that bastard shot Kenny in cold blood, what the hell do I do now James?"

"Take a deep breath John and and try to remain calm." I breath in. "Now let it out slowly, good, now you've got to compose yourself and lead your away team, you can do this Captain."

"You're right Commander." I say taking another deep breath and letting it out slowly, I take a few more breaths and slowly compose myself, then I take stock of the situation. "Admiral Kruel is on his way to the Supernova in my Falcon and he's got about fifty secmen with him. And they are all heavily armed and armoured. So be careful."

"Eye Captain, we will, but don't fret I've got it all covered, they are going to rue the day they messed with the Supernova. Now go be the hero I'm training you to be and rescue the colonists out of the mine and that's an order." Cranky commands with a sheepish grin trying to make light of a bad situation. I try to return the smile but I found no humour after my crewmans grizzly death.

I notice my science officer L.T. Leon Fernandez walking my way and I open up the communication again with visual link to the bridge and my ready room.

"Captain, Commander, You gotta see this." And Leon Fernandez holds up Kenny Kubota's communicator node.

"What did you find Lieutenant?" I ask formally not really in the mood for pleasantries. Leon looks at me with concern and he moves beside me then he brings up the hollow image from the communicator node and starts talking.

"Kenny was running scans of Admiral Kruel before he died and discovered Admiral Kruel's D.N.A. profile. The Admiral is augmented and so are his men." I read along as Leon kept talking. "The D.N.A. Scans Kenny was running proves Berry Lecar is I.R.F. Admiral Victor Kruel. And his ship is the I.R.F. Python. The Admiral and his men have been missing in action for two and a half years

Captain. The I.R.F. Python is also the flagship of the Second I.R.F. Legion." They are also known as the Bravos Exterminatus Corps. Admiral Victor Kruel was augmented in the Eastern Federal Block on Earth. You know what was once the countries in Europe, Asia and Africa?"

"I know where they are Leon, now get to the point!" I order.

"Well, apparently there were only two legions created on Earth. The First I.R.F. Legion in the Western Federal Block and the Second I.R.F. Legion in the East." Said Leon matter of factly.

"Really, I thought all the legions were created on Mars?"

"That's what I thought too, but get this. Both Admirals from the First and Second I.R.F. legions were indoctrinated with the historical leaders that had fought every major battle from there respected Blocks and the Eastern Federal Block has a longer history of warfare and violence than the Western Block does and a darker one too, well, both blocks have a dark past but the East is longer. The fact that the Second I.R.F. Legion has exterminatus added to their unofficial title means that some of the darker military history has come to the forefront of Admiral Kruel's Indoctrination. Also, I think the Admiral is suffering mentaly as well."

"I agree, and we now know that the Twenty Sixth I.R.F. Legion also known as Zulu Company is the only Legion without any reported augmentation psychosis." I say to Cranky and Leon.

Then Cranky pipes in, "And the federation just let the Second I.R.F. Legion go to war knowing about Admiral Kruel's indoctrination and possible psychosis."

"That's right Commander, they did know." Agrees Leon Fernandez.

"Shit, can this get any worse. I say with growing concern.

Leon Frenandez continues talking. "In my medical analysis of this situation we now find ourselves in, I think Admiral Victor Kruel has succumbed to augmentation psychosis."

"I think they all have Lieutenant, good work." And I pat Leon on the back.

"One more thing Captain."

"What's that Leon?" I ask.

"The moment Kenny ran those scans it instantly hit the Intergalactic, Magistrate, Police, Services, data banks. And somehow Kenny Kubota got full access to the entire profile of Admiral Victor Kruel. The Empire sees the Admiral as the galaxy's most dangerous war criminal and we just set foot on the biggest gold nugget in the galaxy and interfered with his plans, not only that, we also let him get away. His past crimes are all here Captain if you wanna know more?"

"Give me the node I'll look at it later." I order and I hold out my hand.

Leon drops the piece of tech in my hand and continues talking. "I think thats why Kenny was killed Captain, Admiral Kruel didn't want you to know that he and his sec-men are I.R.F. and I would bet that the chimps are on there way here now too?"

"That's exactly why Kenny was killed Leon but I also think the Admiral is a very calculating man and somehow we now factor into his grand scheme."

"Ya, one of extermination." Said Leon abrasively.

I shot Leon a look and I comment in contemptment. "If that's the case we would all be dead right now!" Then I noticed Marvin Lewinsky turn around in his chair abruptly.

"Captain it's Marvin sorry to interrupt but we have incoming."

"Who?" I order.

"I was listening to deep space signals again and I found an encrypted transmission from the chimps. Precinct Nine is en-route to our location, it's the Orillian made strike cruiser, dubbed The Hammer of Justice."

Leon just looks at me and shrugs his shoulders in an I told you so manner as he walks away from me. And he makes another comment "Looks like we have another lunatick to deal with. I'm starting to think we have the worst luck in the galaxy Captain."

"Me too Lieutenant, me too."

Ok, here's some more menusha about our empire. The C.H.I.M.P.S. or chimps as I call them. And in case you forgot that's the Cosmic, Highway, Intergalactic, Magistrate, Police, Service. Ya we may poke fun at the acronym and why not it's funny. Thing is these guys are anything but funny. What do you get, If you took the most analretentive people in the galaxy and gave them a badge and then said to them. "Go wage war in the name of justice!" You'd get these guys, the C.H.I.M.P.S.

Fiercely loyal to the Emperor and his regime. Most of the chimps are humans from the planet Orilon, there are some former I.R.F. Troopers among them but not much, however the number is growing. The chimps travel the cosmic highways dealing out their brand of justice in cosmic war ships made in the Orilon sector of space called precincts. These Strike Cruisers are supposedly equipped with non lethal armaments. E.M.P. Devices designed to immobilize rather than destroy. That being said I would wager they have lethal armaments too, and I'm sure they would rather use those in their pursuit of justice. Each precinct houses fifteen hundred people. Five hundred are the ship's crew and one thousand are the cops. It's the Captain that's in charge of his or her precinct and is the one that gives out the orders to hand out justice in the name of the Emperor.

Now Precinct Nine, on the other hand is also frighteningly known throughout the galaxy as the Hammer of Justice and it is captained by a fanatical empirically loyal human from Orilon named Julia Alactus. She is also the daughter of the head of the police service, and he is I.M.P.S. Judge Advocate General, Preator Alactus.

The fact that Captain Julia Alactus is the daughter of the Judge Advocate General, has somehow fed into her brain and she thinks that gives her the right to deal out justice her own way, which is to the extreme, I might add. Julia Alactus does have a boss, another fanatic with ideals about the Empire and she is C.H.I.M.P.S. Commissar Chief Justice Edwardina Erassmus and she is also the head of the chimps, this woman encourages Captain Alactus to use whatever means necessary to get the job done and Captain Julia Alactus has taken police brutality to a whole other level.

If you've done something criminal and Captain Julia Alactus is pursuing you, you'd better pray to whatever God or Gods you worship for a safe passage to heaven or whatever place you think you go to when you die, because you are going there. Even if it's just a small infraction, she may not kill you for something that menial. What she will do however is make you feel her wrath which is as long as the arm of the law itself.

"Ssshit!" I cry out in frustration again. "This is going from bad to worse by the minute. Marvin how long until the Hammer of Justice gets here?"

"We only have thirty four hours Captain."

Then Cranky pipes in once again.

"That seems to be plenty of time to rescue the colonists from the mine, leave this asteroid and be far away from here when Captain Alactus shows up."

"I hope you're right Commander, and good work guys."

"Captain, Charles here I'm sorry for the interruption but Admiral Kruel just made a course correction to the underside of the asteroid, you know, the dark side."

"Yeah, I get it Charles, what the hell is the Admiral doing?" I ask to know one in particular. "Ok Charles run a scan from the shuttle to see why he is headed that way."

"Captain, I'm locked out from all the shuttle's systems."

"Ssshit, is nothing going to go our way? Ok let me think, I've an idea. Charls use the pulsar array and get a three dimensional scan of the asteroid and then feed the image to both mine and Cranky's command nodes."

"Roger that Captain." Obays Charls Vollmer.

"Marvin work with Charles to get it done faster and no bitching about working with Marvin either Charles, got it!"

"Yes sir." Replies Charles in a disappointing tone.

"Ok Captain we are done, whoa looks like there's a ship amalgamated into the asteroid." said the communications officer in amazement.

"Yeah I see it too, good work guys. Commander you thinking what I'm thinking?"

"If you are thinking that that ship is the long lost I.R.F. Python then I will say you are right." Replies Commander James Crane matter of factly.

"Yup the one and only. Ok Commander now why do you suppose the Esteemed Admiral is headed back to his ship? I can think of only one reason how about you?"

"Bloody hell, Admiral Kruel and his men are going for Firehawk gunships." Replies Cranky with concern in his voice.

"Not just any Firehawk gunships Commander, I.R.F. Firehawk gunships. You see ever since Leon gave me Kenny's communicator node I've been looking at all the info on the Python and the rest of the stellar warfleet under the Admiral's command. The Flagship known as the I.R.F. Python is a corvette class carrier, not quite as large as an Orillian strike cruiser mind you, but more devastating because of the Firehawk gunships its loaded with. The only problem with the Emperors warfleet is that it has no carriers or starfighters and every time an Orillian made strike cruiser met an I.R.F. Flagship, it was destroyed by, not only the support ships but mostly by the Firehawk gunships. Each I.R.F. Flagship has two hundred I.R.F. Firehawk gunships on board and the flagships are also supported by two battleship class stellar warships, and the rest of the fleet consists of destroyers. Eventually the Emperor's fleet went after the destroyers leaving only the flag ships exposed to the orillian war fleet. The two supporting battleships in the Second I.R.F. Legion are the I.R.F. Berlin and the I.R.F. Moskow, they are also missing in action as is the rest of the fleet," And that's the problem Commander, Admiral Kruel's fleet is pretty much the only I.R.F. Fleet left and it's still waging war every chance it can get."

"This is very serious indeed Captain. At least we know where the Python is?"

"Right you are Commander, the Python is a carrier and will have lots of I.R.F. Gunships on board which are more like starfighters than shuttles with weapons attached, we must get over there a-sap and commandeer some for ourselves and put a stop to the Admiral before he does something stupid like destroy the Supernova."

"The problem is Skipper, Admiral Kruel has got our bloody shuttle!"

"Captain, I may have a solution to that problem?" Suggests Leon Fernandez looking down at Kenny kubota's corps.

"I'm all ears Lieutenant what do you have in mind?" Then Leon looks up at me and continues.

"Well, when the Admiral lands even if he leaves the shuttle in idle." Then Leon looks back down at Kenny's corps again and trails off bemused by the dead man lying at his feet.

"It turns itself off." Said Jaxina finishing for Leon. "I think I know where he's going with this Captain, the shuttle will actually reset itself to normal protocols when its powering down, giving us access to the shuttle's systems, then we can remotely turn it back on from the Supernova and fly it back here. I'm such an idiot I should've thought of that myself. Very good Lieutenant." Then she gave Leon a love punch to his left shoulder.

"Ouch!" Cries Leon rubbing his shoulder and looking at Jaxina. "Thanks, I think." Then my science officer looks back down at Kenny's corps again still rubbing his shoulder.

"Captain, Don here, I can remotely fly the shuttle over to you once the Admiral lands, we will have to wait a few minutes for the shuttle to reset but I can do this. Said my Helmsman enthusiastically.

"Make it so." I order. "And in the meantime I'll be formulating a plan to get a couple of I.R.F. Gunships for ourselves and rescue the colonists out of the mine. Good work Supernova and stay in touch?"

I look over to where Tyrel Johnson was sitting on the last two steps that led up to the top of the shuttle pad, the former I.R.F. Trooper, had his head in his hands, clearly he was upset about the loss of his friend. I strode over to the young man to offer some condolence not really knowing what to say because Kenny's death has been a shock to me as well.

"You going to be ok son?

"I don't know, Captain, I guess we are calling you that now huh?"

"For the time being. Look son I've never lost a crewman before so don't be upset if I don't know the right words to say to you, but I do know he will be missed. Both you and Kenny work well with my team.

Then Tyrel Johnson Acting Sub Lieutenant Junior Class of the starfreighter known as the Supernova broke down in tears. "He was my best friend Captain, we were like brothers, we grew up together, went to the same schools, played on the same sports teams and when the call came out looking for volunteers for the I.R.F. Legions which was code named the Valhallen Project, Kenny and I signed up. Both Kenny and I survived our augmentation too and when the Federation surrendered a year ago we were given a commission on the Supernova after we registered in the new regime and you just had to bring us with you on this away mission, didn't you, Captain?"

Then Tyrel just looked away from me to stare out at the logistics center with tears rolling down his cheeks.

Right then I knew Tyrel blamed me for Kenny's death. I look away from Tyrel to look at the rest of the crew I was also a little hurt and frustrated and then I order my crew over to me.

"All right everyone around me now!"

They all trot over to me.

"Supernova you listen up too, everyone has a job to do, including me and that also includes you too Acting Sub Lieutenant Johnson and sometimes things go wrong, like what happened to Kenny but that doesn't stop us from completing our mission which is to rescue the colonists." I look down at Tyrel. "Now suck it up Acting Sub Lieutenant and let's do this rescue! Here is the plan. Jaxina you're coming with Tyrel and myself because I'm going to need you to fly the falcon over to the Python when it gets back here." Then Don Watts interrupts.

"You got me Captain I can fly it remotely from the Supernova which I'm doing anyway."

"Sub Lieutenant Watts, your job is to just bring the falcon here and that's it, got it, now zip it!" Also Jaxina you are an accomplished fighter pilot so I need you to fly one of the I.R.F. Gunships." I look over at Lee Oswald now. "Lieutenant Commander you're in charge of finding and releasing the colonists from the mines."

"Roger that Captain." Replies Lee.

I look back down at Tyrel and he was still looking out over the colony as tears continued to fall down his cheeks.

"I wanna go with the Lieutenant Commander." He finally says to me.

"Fine, Jaxina looks like it's just you and me."

"Roger that Captain, and no funny business, we are on duty after all." She then lowers her aviators to give me a serious look and then a playful wink while chewing a mouthful of nicotine gum.

I know she was trying to cheer me up but I found no humor, I had for all intensive purposes just shut myself off of emotion and I was all business now. I give her a stern look and I comment. "Now is not the time Sub Lieutenant."

I look over to my science officer Lieutenant Leon Fernandez whom was looking down at Kenny Kubota's corps in morbid fascination and again I make a comment of my own to my crewman.

"Do you see something you like? You have not stopped staring at his corps since he died man, Leon!"

"Yeah." Is all he says to me as he looks up at me in bewilderment.

"You're going with the Lieutenant Commander." I gesture toward Lee Oswald.

"What about Kenny? Leon asks looking down again and pointing to the dead man. "We can't just leave him here."

"We will take his body back with us once we complete this mission." I reply.

"Who the hell is Kenny by the way?" Demands Lee Oswald.

"If you are joking right now?" I say pointing at the Lieutenant Commander. "It's not funny."

"Yeah, what the hell!" Replies Jaxina while crossing her arms and giving Lee a distasteful look.

"Are you kidding me dumbass?" Leon says still pointing at Kenny's corps. "The man who is lying dead on the ground, right there, the guy that was covering your back this entire time before he died, you pendejo puta brain."

"Leon that's enough!" I order.

"Yeah, that's enough." Orders Lee Oswald.

"That'll be all outta you too Oswald!" I demand.

"What did I do?" Questions Lee defensively. "Sooo his name is Kenny?"

"Yes!" We all say together.

"You know I'm not very good with names only faces and that dead body has no face. I'm sorry I just can't identify it."

I roll my eyes and grunt out in frustration. "For the love of the cosmos man!" Then I bring up Kenny Kubota's I.D. Picture and send it to Lieutenant Commander Lee Oswald's H.U.D.

"Oh hey look its Kenny Kubota, good kid, he will make a fine addition to my security team on the Supernova. Wait a minute."

I grunt in frustration again and beary my face in my right hand just shaking my head all the while Lee Oswald was still talking.

"It says here he is K.I.A. Killed in action." Then the Lieutenant Commander looks down at the corps lying on the ground and then he looks back at me and asks "That's Kenny Kubota then?" I just nod my head. Then Lieutenant Commander Lee Oswald did something I will never forget, the big man looks back at the corps, kneels down and pulls a Federation I.R.F. Unit flag from somewhere in his backpack and drapes it over Kenny Kubota's body covering up the bloody mess and gore. Then Lieutenant Commander Lee Oswald hung his head in a moment of silence for the deceased man. Lee then stands up and looks at all of us studying us one by one and comments.

"It's the only thing I had to cover his body with, it's the old standard of my unit when I was in the I.R.F. If you all got something better to cover his body with, then by all means use it." He orders Tyrel and Leon to fall in behind him, he looks at me and in a serious tone and makes another comment.

"I'm going to look for the colonists now, I'll inform you once I've rescued them, assuming they still live."

And with that the augmented human that is Lieutenant Commander Lee Oswald and the head of my security on the Supernova trotted off toward the outer colony, leaving Jaxina and myself alone with one another.

As we watch the rescue team disappear into the obscure distance of the logistics center, Jaxina pipes up.

"You do know he will get the job done with professional ease right?"

"Yes he will Jaxina, yes he will." I reply, still watching the team shrink in the distance beyond the containers and machinery while Jaxina continues talking.

"It's just that he seems a bit off his rocker at times do you know what I mean Captain?"

"I do Jaxina and I think it's due to the stresses of being augmented, don't worry he's mostly in control of his mental state, he just shakes and gets migraines once in awhile. He also has an uncontrollable urge to give us all a lecture on gun safety before we disembark from the shuttle when we are on away missions, he always does that."

"Tell me about it, I know more about my side arm now than I did when weapon safety was a class at the starfighter academy."

"Ha ha I know. I say chuckling and agreeing with the beautiful pilot standing beside me whom was also looking out at the shrinking team.

"You know something Captain? He is very loyal to you."

"I know and we were a bit hard on him."

"More like Fernandez you mean, and what the hell is a pendejo puta brain anyway?" She asks looking at me with a questioning glare.

"Don't look at me!" I plead. "How the hell should I know!"

"Captain your shuttle is here." Blurts out Don Watts over the comms.

Then Cranky interrupts.

"You know Skipper, you should have roped in your crew a little better than that. Lieutenant Fernandez was bit insubordinate on Lieutenant Commander Oswald.

"Cranky if I wanted a lecture on insubordination I'd have gone to one of your study groups, now can it!"

"Wow, wish I could talk to him like that." Said Jaxina with a chuckle in her voice while we ascended the stairs to the top of the shuttle pad.

"You can it too woman." I say to her jokingly.

Jaxina suddenly stops before she gets to the top of the stairs, she turns around and sticks her tongue out at me.

"Ya, ya, go on get up there." I say smiling and glad that the beautiful pilot is still trying to keep my spirits up.

As Jaxina and I crest the top of the stairs my Falcon Class Shuttle arrives blowing heated wind about us from the landing thrusters.

"Good job Don, Jaxina's got it from here."

"Yes sir, have fun, you know I can."

"Zip it Watts, the answer is no!"

"Fine." Is all my helmsman says to me.

"Persistent isn't he." Comments Jaxina.

"Hey you be quiet!" Orders Don.

"The both of you knock it off and that's an order!" I command to Don and Jaxina.

"Yes sir." They both say together.

"Charles, feed the shuttle the course change to its computer so Jaxina has a way point.

"Roger that Captain, there you go Jaxina it's all set."

"Thank you Charles."

A moment later Jaxina and I settled into our seats aboard the cockpit of the Falcon, she runs her fingers over the touchpad controls and we lift off.

"Jaxina, I know you've flown a Firehawk gunship before?" I ask the beautiful pilot. "But the question remains are you going to be able to fly an I.R.F. Firehawk gunship?"

"Why is something different?"

"Yup and thanks to Kenny running scans of the Admiral with his communicator node, I now have the full specs of the I.R.F. Starfighter because that's what it really is a starfighter and not a gunship despite the fact that it's called a gunship. Here let me send you those specs via our nodes so you can familiarise yourself with the workings of this beauty."

"Woa this thing is hard core, it says here that it can only be flown by a single pilot?" She looks at me questionly.

That's why you are with me I wanted Tyrel here too because he can fly as well but I don't think he wants to be around me right now." Then I look at her with a smile and I pop the question. "Jaxina would you like to have an I.R.F. Firehawk gunship of your own?"

She looks at me in amazement mouth agape and starts talking once again "You're mad, you really think we will be able to hide some of these starfighters aboard the Supernova out of the eyes of the chimps, they do level one inspections on star freighters all the time, one thousand chimps will combe every inch of the Supernova, inside and out?"

"I know they will, but I know where to hide the gunships."

"Captain I know you're ambitious and all but I did not know you are crazy, this is piracy this is illegal we are not allowed to carry military equipment."

"Sometimes Sub Lieutenant you've got to resort to piracy to get the job done in the pursuit of justice and don't worry I take full responsibility if we get caught and we are not going to get caught."

"Ok Captain, you're the one in charge, but do you think we can pull this off before the chimps get here?"

"I do, and all you have to worry about is taking out the Admiral and his men when the opportunity arises. Also try not to kill the Admiral if you have him in your sights we need him alive. His men on the other hand I give you full permission to use lethal force against them. I know you can do this Jaxina you're an excellent pilot an ace even. Your combat record proves this."

"Right Captain." She says letting out a deep breath. "Let's do this." And we accelerate toward the darkside of the asteroid.

We disembark from the Falcon in total darkness after we land and the only thing that was visible was the area the spotlights of the shuttle craft exposed. The lights were aimed on the hull of a massive war ship exposing a huge gaping hole that could be seen in the illumination. Above the breach in large black letters was the name of the ship, I.R.F. Python.

"Looks like that's our way in Sub Lieutenant, ladies first." I gesture toward the breach with a slight chivalric bow.

"Oh my hero you are so kind." She says teasing me then my beautiful pilot gets serious. "I wish I had a weapon."

"Ya me too Jax me too.

"Captain, Marvin here."

"Go ahead Marv, what's up?"

"I just picked up a transmission from inside the Python."

"What the hell, from who?"

"Here I'll just play it for you Captain it is addressed to you after all."

"Really?"

"Captain John Mott of the Nova-Tech Corporation Starfreighter Supernova. I'm Master Chief Danny Reese, head of colony security here on Midas Eighty Eight. Do you copy? I repeat. Do you copy?"

"Marvin can he hear me?" I ask

"Yes he can hear you."

"As a matter of fact I can hear you Captain, It would seem you have a very skilled communications officer."

"No shit, good work Marvin. So tell me Master Chief what the hell happened? How did you end up inside the Python and not out here trying to protect the colony?"

I heard the Master Chief sigh in frustration and then he told me the whole events that had transpired right up until I showed up.

"After the colony was built, the Federation was the one that provided the law enforcement and security for Midas Eighty Eight. I was a Lieutenant in the F.A.F. You know the Federal Armed Forces. I was eventually transferred to the F.A.F. Special Forces and after some top secret training I was given a promotion to Master Chief and a new commission to be the head of security on a new colony. I was also told by my superiors that I would have a full company of troops at my command. It took three weeks to get here from Mars and by the time my troops and I arrived, the mining operation was in full swing. The first year here was uneventful, then Orilon declared war on the Federation and that's when things changed. This war started because the Emperor found out about this mining colony. Did you know this asteroid is eighty eight million metric tons of gold?"

"Holy shit, really?" I reply in shocked amazement.

"Yes Captain it's true, now back to what I was saying. A few weeks after the Emperor's declaration of war was announced all over the galaxy we got our first high ranking visitor to the colony."

"Let me guess, I.R.F. Admiral Victor Kruel?"

"The one and only, Captain, but he was much more diplomatic and respectful, professional even. That first meeting with Dr. Midal I attended as well. The Admiral said that he was taking charge of the colony under strict orders from the leaders of the Federation and who was I too argue, Victor Kruel is a full admiral of the Federation and a leader of an I.R.F. Legion to boot. I'm only an F.A.F. Special Forces Master Chief, I'm not even that anymore because the Federation surrendered a year ago. At any rate, Admiral Kruel turned this place into an I.R.F. Stronghold and his base of operations. I remained the head of security while the Admiral ran his campaign from the same office complex. He even commissioned ten thousand Firehawk gunships and put them on board his entire fleet because they don't need launch tubes to get into the action it was a stroke of military genius. The Admiral kept the Python close by in case the colony was attacked, which it was for a while. Having all those regular Firehawk gunships on every ship in his fleet has been the reason his fleet is still waging war and why Admiral Kruel is considered the most dangerous war criminal in the galaxy. The I.M.P.S. and it's two branches are even afraid of Admiral Victor Kruel. So the Emperor turned his attention away from this asset because that is what Midas Eighty Eight is, an asset of insurmountable wealth. And he focused his war efforts into destroying the rest of the Federation's Military and he did just that leaving Admiral Kruel to defend this colony and then the Emperor committed his entire fleet to destroying Admiral Kruel. And his highness is slowly decimating the Second I.R.F. Legion every chance they get. But Admiral Kruel is very clever and considered a military genius."

"That is the reason why the Admiral's still alive isn't it Master Chief?"

"That would be my guess Captain and not only that he is ruthless and I'm also surprised that you are all still alive as well and not dead like your crewman."

"Me too Master Chief, me too."

"As I was saying, shortly after the Federation surrendered we got our second high ranking visitors to Midas Eighty Eight and how they got through the blockade remains a mystery. It was the Royal Emissary with his retinue from Orilon and this time both Admiral Kruel and I were not invited to the meeting with Dr Roger Midal. Papers were signed as well as a declaration stating that the colony is now under the jurisdiction of the empire and all citizens of the colony must register under the new regime including all former

F.A.F. military personnel and all I.R.F. Legionnaires. That drove the Admiral nuts and to commit murder, he killed the Emissary and his people, Dr. Roger Midal, as well as the planetary governor because he thought they were traitors. My men and I fought back and eventually we had to surrender too we were just out numbered.

The colonists were rounded up and put in the mines and what remains of my men and I were escorted at gunpoint put on a shuttle and flown to the Python and after that I don't know what happened because I woke up and bulkheads were smashed and destroyed and I could tell the Python was a wreck. And I've been locked away inside engineering with a handful of my men and about fifty engineers since Admiral Kruel's uprising and now here you are attempting a rescue and messing up the Admirals plans which is working by the way. Tell you what you get us outta here and my men and I will help you take down the Admiral and his sec-men what do you say, can you help us Captain?"

"Ya, Jaxina and I will try to get you all free. Don I want you to fly the engineers to the Supernova once we free everyone from their entrapment and then fly the Falcon back to the logistics center."

"Roger that Captain."

"And Cranky put the engineers to work on fixing the engines of the Supernova and give them all commissions too."

"Eye Skipper."

"So tell me Master Chief what are we going to find when we get in there?" I ask while moving into the massive breach of the huge war ship.

"Probably a lot of dead bodies, destroyed equipment, carnage mostly, that sort of thing."

"Am I going to have a run in with the Admiral and his men because Jaxina and I have no weapons?"

"Probably not Captain they should've all taken flight in Firehawks by now. Tell me Captain are you and Sub Lieutenant Jaxina Bernardino in the ship now?"

"Yes we are, why?"

"Because I'm going to let the chief engineer guide you to engineering he knows more about the Python than I do."

"That makes sense."

Jaxina and I made our way cautiously through the wreckage of the Python toward engineering with the chief engineer giving us directions. We scoured the decks of the war ship looking for safe passage to engineering and the first thing we came across while we slowly made our way through the damaged bulkheads was the armoury.

"Well, well looks like we found the armoury." I say while I open the door to the room beyond to reveal a cache of weapons inside.

"Lee is going to love this place. You are going to tell him about it aren't you Captain?" Asks Jaxina.

"Bloody rights I am, but I also wanna check it out and catalogue everything that's in here so Lee can pick what he wants to take with him back to the Supernova."

"Good idea Captain." She says approvingly.

As soon as Jaxina and I entered the room the ark lights lit up the place and the two of us were not disappointed, firearms of all types filled the wall racks around the big room and shelves of armour filled up the space between the four walls from floor to ceiling. I grab another P4 ion shot blaster gun off the wall and stuff it in my holster and Jaxina did the same as well, I felt much better now that I had a side arm once again. I also grabbed a few magazine batteries or mag-batts as we call them for my side arm as well. I touch the command node on my wrist and I scan the room to catalogue the weapons for inventory on the Supernova. I also sent Lee directions leading right to the armoury.

Once I was done my scan of the room Jaxina and I left the Armoury and we were guided once again to engineering by the Chief Engineer. We arrived a little while later and found the door to engineering blocked by a damaged bulkhead.

"Looks like a massive bulkhead blocks the way to engineering I don't think we can move this, it's a solid mess." I say in a disappointing tone.

"I was afraid of that Captain that had to be the handy work of the Admiral."

"Don't worry Master Chief, Jaxina and I have got this, we are both excellent pilots." I say with a hint of machismo in my voice.

"You sure you can fly an I.R.F. Firehawk gunship Captain?"

"Whom do you think was the helmsman of the Supernova for the last twenty years Master Chief."

"Realy?"

"It's true, I flew it all back then for Lord Holland Monical an Orillian diplomat involved in establishing a proper trade network for the Orilon Empire. He started his corporation by having the Supernova built during Orilon's dark period. Then the war started, man, we had a lot of close calls going through the blockades, good thing Lord Monical was captain of the Supernova back then because we flew back and forth between the Orilon system and the Sol system a lot during the war. Lord Monical's title saved us numerous times from attack from both sides because he was also commissioned by the federation as well to keep trade going from the Sol system to Orilon. Lord Monical deceived both the Empire and the Federation into thinking that he was loyal to each other,so he got contracts to ship cargo from one system to the other and back, bloody brilliant having documentation to ship cargo for both sides and a Lordship entitlement as well. Then his Lordship's corporation just got to large and he needed to step away from the Supernova, he tried making Commander Crane the Captain but Cranky would have none of it so he made me the man in charge and I've been Captain ever since and that was four years ago"

"What were the documentation that Lord Monical manage to use to cross the blockades?" Asked the Master Chief caught up in the story.

"Oh, bills of lading." I replied matter of factly.

"What the hell is that?" Asks Danny Reese.

"Bills of lading are legal binding documentation that has all the information about the cargo that is being shipped and third party liability laws that protect the shipper and also the freight company and the company that receives the cargo as well. It aso entrusts that the conveyance of said cargo will therefore be shipped in a timely and safe manor by the freighter entrusted with the cargo. If the cargo gets damaged during said conveyance and can be proven then the freight company is responsible for the damaged cargo."

"What if the shipper damages the cargo when they are loading and the freighter personne_ can prove it?" Asks the Master Chief.

"Then the Captain of said freighter has the right to refuse the cargo and then it's the responsibility of the shipper to fix the damaged goods being loaded same thing if the receiver damages the cargo. That being said if foreign entities not on the bill of lading manage to steal or damage said cargo then a criminal investigation will take place and if the foreign entities are caught they will be fined and or imprisoned and no side wanted that kind of legal ramification while they were making war with each other, so they let us through the blockades every time."

"Ha Ha, nice."

"And if I can catch the Admiral he will have one more felony to answer for and this time it won't be a war crime but the damage of cargo destined for Orion Station. Well looks like you and your friends have to find another way out I'm sorry Master Chief we won't leave you stranded here either you have my word, It would have been nice to have your support out there."

"Eye Captain and good luck out there."

"Thanx Master Chief, Jaxina it's up to us to take down the Admiral."

"I'm with you Captain, looks like I'm your wing-girl after all."

"I wouldn't have it any other way."

"Captain when this is over you are going to buy me a drink."

"I will definitely buy you that drink when this is over. You know Jaxina this qualifies as our first date."

She looks at me incredulously and smirks or smiles I'm not really sure which because in the dim illumination of our helmet lamps she looked so beautiful and I was entranced in the moment.

'For the love of the cosmos she is sexy.' I thought to myself as I fumbled for the communications button on the command node on my wrist.

"Marvin link communications with engineering on the Python and assign Jaxina and myself a Firehawk gunship each."

"Roger that Captain, wait, did you just say to assign you a Firehawk as well?"

"Yes I did Lieutenant."

"Just do it Lewinsky!" Yells Commander James Crane A.K.A. Cranky, my first officer on the Supernova. Then he asks me a question.

"Are you ready for this Captain, this is no simulation?"

"I'm well aware of that fact James now zip it because you're distracting me and I'm trying to formulate a plan. Charles plot a course through the asteroid field and send it to my helmet's H.U.D. and I'll upload it to my Hawk's computer then I want you to flag the Admiral and his squadron. Also can someone give us directions again so we can get to our launch tubes?"

Once again the chief engineer of the I.R.F. Python sent us toward our assigned launch tubes and again it was slow going because of all the wreckage that we had to climb over and under just to get to the hangar area.

We finally arrived at the launch tube bay and Jaxina and I, had company. Two of the Admiral's henchmen had waited behind in case we were ambitious enough to try and get our hands on the I.R.F. Firehawk gunships. Which we were, I was glad for the fact that I had rearmed myself in the armoury because the two henchmen wasted no time in trying to kill the both of us.

The two jerks in the room beyond the doorway had fortified themselves behind some equipment crates and opened fire as soon as we made ourselves known. Ion shots are lethal to organics such as us humans, luckily we cover ourselves in hard suits and the tungsten ark material that make up each round did not penetrate our hard suits or the steel bulkheads as we leapt for cover.

Jaxina took cover behind the wall on the left side of the open doorway to the launch tub bay and I was taking cover beside her on the other wall.

"Hey Master Chief I thought you said that there would be nobody here?" I asked over the cacophony of gunfire.

"How was I to know the Admiral would leave a rear guard, I told you he was clever."

"Don't worry Captain I got this." I look over at Jaxina and she held a grenade in her hand.

"It's an ark grenade, don't look in the doorway when it goes off otherwise you will go blind for a while and you need your eyesight."

"Where did you get that?" I ask in amazement.

"From the armoury of course, Captain I need you to start firing at them to suppress them so they don't see me lob the grenade through the door, there is a gap between the two equipment crates that they are hiding behind just wide enough to fit the grenade and when this bad boy goes off they will be stunned into submission because the ark tech in the grenade will immobilize there I.R.F. Implants indefinitely."

"Good thinking Jax, give me the word when you're ready?"

"Start firing Captain!" She yells to me.

"I poke my head out just enough to get a look at the henchmen and I start firing. Immediately they take cover behind their makeshift fortifications and still, I keep squeezing the trigger.

"Fire in the hole!" Jaxina yells, I have just enough time to see her grenade bounce on the floor and land in the gap. And luckily as I ducked my head back behind cover it goes off.

Jaxina and I hear the two I.R.F. Troopers yell in pain as the ark technology in the grenade shoots bolts of lightning strait at the two henchmen and all around them, it also electrifies them both internally and when the yelling stopped and the bright blue light of the ark-tech went out, we poked our heads out through the door and all was silent.

Jaxina draws her side arm, another P4 ion shot blaster gun and we both move in either directions out the door while our blaster guns were trained on the spot where the two henchmen were taking cover, we cautiously move up the flanks to the subdued troopers, I kneel down and check for lifesigns and found none.I look up at Jaxina and comment.

"Well, they are both dead Jim." I say in my best Dr McCoy. "Looks like the ark grenade did more than just immobilize them."

"I wasn't trying to kill them Captain you gotta believe me, I just wanted to immobilize them I didn't know the ark grenade would kill them, honestly Captain I didn't know and stop making fun, I'm being serious."

"I believe you Jaxina." I say while I stood up and holster my blaster gun. "Just take a deep breath and let it out slowly and remain calm we still have a job to do can I trust you to fly?'

"Yes Captain you can, thank you. Then my personal pilot takes in a deep breath and lets it out. "I'll be fine now, lets go kick some ass!"

"That's my girl."

I sat in the seat of the cockpit of my I.R.F. Firehawk gunship, I pull off my helmet and place it in a slot down by my feet and once I entered the command sequence into the gunships computer my helmet's heads up display transferred to the Firehawks computer and the plex steel glass canopy became my H.U.D. All comms via my command link in my hardsuit's helmet transferred to the gunship's computer, as well as my Identification. Then the I.R.F. Firehawk gunship known as the Vengeance of Europa became my starfighter.

"Captain you're not going to believe this, I have a bit of a problem."

"What's up Jaxina?"

I hear her sigh in frustration and a nanosecond later she tells me what her problem is

"The name of my Firehawk has just changed from the Wild Rose to… To…uhgh."

"Just tell me Sub Lieutenant." I demand.

"Fine, it's changed from the Wild Rose to the Mork from Ork and now I have a password to start her and I'm locked out if I don't type it and say it at the same time."

"I start laughing, Bob it has to be Bob he's gotten into my classic T.V. Shows again."

"I'm going to kill him, dambit Bob!" She yells. I see her hit her consul. "Nanu nanu!" Yells my wing-girl and a nanosecond later she launches.

"A microsecond after Jaxina launches I launch too. The reverse singularity maglens powers up the kinetic barrier while the ark tech in conjunction with the kinetic barrier and my launch thrusters slingshots my Firehawk gunship out the launch tube.

"Nanu nanu!" I yell as I race down the launch tube. I reversed the thrusters the moment I exited the Python. The velocity is so great that you only have nanoseconds to get control of your vector. With Charls navigation calculations uploaded to our heads up displays, Jaxina and I were able to make our way safely out the asteroid field and race away toward the Supernova, free of debris doing a hyper sonic velocity equivalent to mach ten.

"Ok Sub Lieutenant listen up, there's a big possibility that the Admiral and his men know we are coming, likewise he may not, two things are going to happen: One when we get close to the squadron it may be a trap to lure us in leaving our flanks exposed on both sides. There are three squads in the main formation out there."

"I see them Captain." Adds Jaxina.

"Good, each fighter squadron will compose of five fighters. Two fighters from the outside squads should break formation to come around and flank us from behind, watch for that break and we will take out as many as we can of the remaining formation before we are targeted from the flanking fighters."

"The second thing that might happen is that the Admiral and his men might not even know that we even launched from the Python and then we have the drop on him. And we're close enough we give them all the fire power we can muster. And if I do have any luck the Master Chief and the rest of his men will rendezvous with us, assuming they can find a way out of engineering."

"I don't like our odds Captain, the two of us against fifteen fighters?"

"Never tell me the odds Sub Lieutenant, never tell me the odds. Ok Supernova, light up the hostiles inbound to your location. Tag all the squad leaders in yellow, tag all support fighters in red and tag the Admiral in blue."

"Roger that Skipper." I see Cranky whirl around and start barking his order at Marvin Lewinsky. "You heard the man get it done!"

A few seconds later, yellow and red dots appeared on my heads up display. "Good work Supernova."

"Captain I don't see the Admiral's fighter in my heads up display at all." Said Jaxina in a somewhat puzzled voice.

"Nor do I Sub Lieutenant, lets not worry about the Admiral for now, let's concentrate on the squadrons first. "I sure wish I had some of those E.M.P. Weapons the chimps use." I said thinking out loud. And then something truly bizarre happened.

Captain this is Head Arkanologist Lucreasha Millenius speaking.

"Madam Millenius, what are you doing on the bridge? The Supernova is under a state of emergency and you know that the only people that are allowed on the bridge during an emergency are the bridge crew."

"Captain, I have been in your waiting room all day, which is considered part of the bridge so I decided to see what was taking so long and here I stand watching the ship's captain try to be a super-hero. You do know today is my monthly meeting with you, or did you forget?"

That was today? I'm sorry, Madam Millenius but as you can see I have been really busy with this emergency situation. Now what can I do for you?"

I watch Madam Millenius fold her arms and give me a motherly stern look of contemptment and then she comments.

"Yes, I see that, busy saving the day once again and rushing headlong into danger. Well Captain, I do not approve of this behavior from our commanding officer, even though you continue to do so against my council, however, that being said. I may have a way that you can get the E.M.P. weapons you desire."

"You do, really, how?" I ask somewhat puzzled.

"Through arkanology of course." She said matter of factly.

"Um, ok." I reply dumbfounded.

"Trust me Captain it will work I just have to send you the right sequences of programed codes via the command network and your hardsuit will do the rest. Your hardsuit's command link will be the key. I've been formulating a new theory through arkanology for a while now and this seems like the perfect time to test this theory."

"This sounds bad, why am I always the guinea pig in all of your new theories?" I ask with a hint of panic in my voice.

"Because your the Captain." She answers back.

I don't know If Madam Millenius was being literal or sarcastic, because as I've mentioned before the woman's odd and I can't tell one way or the other.

"Trust me Captain, this won't hurt a bit, really, I swear to you. Your hardsuit is made with ark technology when it was constructed and so is your Firehawk, that's all I need for this to work. You are also, already linked together with the Supernova, therefore all I need to do is send you my coded language of arkanology across your command link. Then you will be able to switch between E.M.P. And lethal armaments at a push of a button on your flight consul."

"Wow, that's unbelievable, you can do that?" I say with some skepticism.

"Yes, Captain I can do that, but you have to trust me."

"I know this arkcanology can do amazing things but that just seems impossible." I say with more skepticism.

"I know how it sounds, just let me try. I also know you don't want to kill anybody out there. Will you let me try this Captain?"

Then Jaxina interrupts.

"We are fifteen hundred killometeres and closing Captain. Still no sign of the Admiral."

"Ok Madam Millenius, lets try it. I demand.

"Here goes Captain." I see Arkanist Millenius produce some sort of a device from a pocket in her formal robes of office. She then hovers her left hand over the device and produces a bolt of lightning strait in to the device from her hand.

"Lieutenant Marvin Lewinsky do not open the files that I'm uploading to your communications consul, just send them straight to Captain Mott and that's an order young man!"

I smirk as Marvin gets issued an order from somebody else other than me and Cranky.

"Yes mam." Marvin says a little deflated as he follows her orders.

A nano second later after I open Madam Millenius's files, my whole body lit up in static electricity, archaic symbols appeared all over in my heads up display and my flight consul went from the orange glow of the holographic touch display to a soft aqua blue. A transformation took place too, a new armament display appeared to my right just in reach of my index finger.

Then something else happened, this is the bizarre part, well, actually the whole thing was bizarre but this was the really bizarre part. I blacked out for a nano or two and I heard a voice in my head, it was not malevolent nor benevolent in fact it held no emotion at all and all it said was, Captain Mott.

As I was coming back to reality I heard Jaxina yelling over the coms and I notice that we had come up on the three squadrons of the Admiral's fighters unawares.

"Captain, can you hear me? What just happened? Your Firehawk just transformed a bit, the wing span just grew two more meters on either side and you now have more missiles underneath the wings!"

"Ya Jaxina, I now have the E.M.P. Weapons that I wished for. Thank You Madam Millenius that was incredible."

"You are welcome Captain, now hurry up so we can have our meeting."

"Yes mam." I reply.

"Captain that was incredible do you think Madam Millenius can do that for my Firehawk too?"

"Yes my dear I will do the same for you, just give me a nano, Marvin you know what to do?"

"Yes mam." replies my communications officer.

Again, I notice Arkanist Millenius produce a bolt of lightning into her device.

"There you go Miss Bernardino you are all set."

"Thank you Madam Millenius."

"You are welcome my dear."

I look over to my wing-girl's Firehawk and watch in total disbelief as lightning encircles her entire gunship and the wingspan grow two more meters on either side, new missiles hung below as well. I know what your thinking too, how the hell did that happen, ya right not bloody likely, but I saw with my own eyes the transformation to Jaxina's gunship. This arkanology or ark-technology or whatever it is, is something that I cannot begin to fathom and don't ask me to explain it either because I don't know how it works.

"This is unbelievable Captain, I don't understand what just happened, but now I Have E.M.P. armaments too."

"That's great Sub Lieutenant, now cut the chatter, we will discuss this later. Nine oclock incoming." I say in my most commanding voice.

"I see them Captain."

"We have the advantage, now engage!"

"By your command!"

'Ha, she's been into my classic T.V. Shows again.' I thought. "Break right!" I order.

My wing-girl and I break right and open fire with our new electromagnetic ballistic cannons. Or E.M.B. Cannons. These E.M.B. Rounds are shield busters and having them In my arsenal is now my advantage. In our opening salvo Jaxina and I immobilise seven fighters leaving only eight left. The enemy squadron breaks left and Jaxina and I come around to our three oclock to engage the fighters trying to flank us. Now the dog fight begins as three more enemy fighters break formation to flank us once again. My wing-girl and I did not hesitate, we open fire and take out two more leaving them dead in space. The three remaining fighters in formation opens up hell and depletes my shields by twenty percent leaving, seventy percent shield capacity left as they rocket past Jaxina and I.

I look in my rear view and notice the three fighters that had fired upon us break to their right and come around for another pass.

"All right Jaxina there is only six fighters left, you break left and I will break right and we'll head them off at the pass, good luck Sub Lieutenant."

"Roger that Captain and good luck as well."

I come out of my turn with full turbo thrust and I engage my hyper velocity assault on the three fighters now coming at me and I open fire. "That's one down." I say to know one in particular. I perform a barrel roll as the enemy starts firing and as I reach the apex of the roll, I take out the middle fighter and as I was coming out of the roll I took out the remaining fighter. Yes I was hit too and my shields got depleted down to twenty percent capacity. With my three enemies down I decided to go help Jaxina.

"Could use a little help here Captain." she demands as if reading my mind.

"Hang in there Sub Lieutenant, I'm on my way!"

"I can't shake this fighter off me and I'm down to thirty percent shield capacity you gotta take him out Captain, twenty five percent now!"

Somehow one of the three fighters that Jaxina was going after got in behind her, and was making mince meat out of her shields. I come upon the enemy I.R.F. Firehawk gunship and I open fire, nothing, I had depleted the E.M.B. Cannons on my Firehawk and I had no choice but to switch to lethal weapons to save my wingman, Sub Lieutenant Jaxina Bernardino.

Once again I open fire and long blue streams of light hits the enemy in front of me, I was targeting his turbo thrusters when the fighter's aft shields disintegrated and I was rewarded with an explosion as the thruster engine went nuclear. I was also expecting ion shots and not lasers. I guess Madam Millenius's arkanology also created laser cannons in place of my Firehawks ion cannons. This was my first use of energy weapons that I've heard so much about. This is also my first confirmed kill during this whole operation which I was not happy about as well. I did not want to kill anyone, I want justice, not a death sentence, that sentence is reserved for the Admiral alone, not his men.

"Thanks Captain that was close."

"Your welcome Jaxina, how much shield capacity do you have left?" I ask concerned.

"I'm down to fifteen percent shield capacity, Captain, why do you ask?

"Because I've got that bad feeling in my gut again."

"Oh, oh, I hate it when you say that because it means something bad is going to happen. Wait, why do I see four more squadrons coming out of the asteroid field?"

"Because Jaxina we aren't out of the proverbial woods just yet, looks like Marvin made a proximity field around the Supernova and extended it all the way to Midas Eighty Eight anythig entering this sector will be lit up."

"Good work Marvin."

"Indeed, hold on I see Admiral Kruel amongst the squadron."

"Ya I see him too but where did they all come from Captain?"

"I bet one of the I.R.F. Battle ships is around here somewhere." I say with ever growing concern.

"This is bad Captain the Supernova doesn't stand a chance against an I.R.F. Battleship."

"I know Jaxina, but we can't worry about that right now because the enemy fighters are really close. What do you have for weapons?"

"My E.M.B. cannons are depleted but I've got lasers and rockets and that's it."

"Ya me too, so I guess we are going hot from here on in."

"Roger that Captain, switching to lasers now."

"No, switch to long range while we have the chance and let loose our rockets." I order.

"Ok,Captain."

"I got target lock, on three fighters how about you Jax?"

"I got four Captain."

"Good, now let loose." I order once again.

I was surprised by the fact that we took out seven fighters again with our rockets and another surprising fact was that the enemy Firehawks were not the I.R.F. model Firehawk gunships either, there was indeed a battleship in the area.

Jaxina and I were also rewarded with three more kills each when we switched over to our laser cannons. These blue streams of lethal light make short work of the enemy fighters, but we did not come out of that last salvo unscathed either, my bird took a beating and so did Jaxina when we performed our evasive maneuvers.

"There is far to many of them Captain and my shields are out any more hits and I'm done for."

"Ya me too Jaxina." I say as we keep heading away from the enemy squadron. Then my heart sank in my chest as I saw another squadron of fighters closing in on us at hyper speed.

"I don't have any rockets left, all I got are my laser cannons Captain what do we do?"

"Open fire!" I order.

"With pleasure Captain I'm not going down without a fight."

"Neither am I Sub Lieutenant neither am I."

"Wait Captain don't fire It's me, Lieutenant Commander Lee Oswald I brought company."

"I see that, aren't you supposed to be rescuing the civilians?"

"I did Captain and I Left Leon in charge of getting the people off the asteroid."

"You were supposed to let me know when you successfully rescued the civilians."

"Captain, you and Jaxina were busy taking out that first squad of I.R.F. Firehawk gunships, which was expertly done by the way, so I told Commander Crane instead and he gave me the order to go find a way to get the Master Chief out of engineering on the Python and thanks to your directions to the armoury the chief of engineering was able to lead me and Acting Sub Lieutenant Johnson to engineering."

"How did you get them out Lee?"

"Tyrel and I smashed our way through the bulkhead that was blocking the way into engineering."

"Wow, augmented superhuman strength, good work guys and Cranky, it's about time you made a commanding decision on your own. There was a slight pause of dead air as we waited for the sarcastic remark from Commander Crane. "He's not listening in on the command link is he?" I inquire a moment later.

"No Captain, it seems he's got it turned off and it looks like he's chastising Marvin about something again as well." Replied Lieutenant Commander Lee Oswald.

"Speaking of the armoury did you get any new weapons?"

"Uh, Captain no time to chat we have in coming and I'm taking the lead on this, you and Jaxina fall back, you are no good to me without any shields and we all can't afford to lose our commanding officer. Master Chief send a couple of your men to stay with the Captain and Sub Lieutenant Bernardino for protection, in case another squad comes out of nowhere." He orders

"Roger that Lieutenant Commander." Replies Master Chief Danny Reese.

"Marvin light up all friendly Firehawks in green and tag our names and rank on each friendly bird." I order. "And Cranky leave Marvin alone."

I heard a lot of praise from the Master Chief and his men when there heads up displays lit up with all the friendly Firehawks.

"This will make things so much easier." Said Master Chief Danny Reese and he continued to talk while engaging the enemy. "You know Captain you and your crew are quite surprising, I can't tell if you guys are totally crazy thrill seekers or that you have all become so skilled in combat because you all get into situations that end up in battles."

Then something funny happens.

"We all get into situations that ends up in battles." We all say together to Danny Reese.

"We don't go looking for trouble Master Chief trouble just seems to find us every time we get an S.O.S. And that's why we've become skilled in dealing with said trouble.

"Captain, all enemy fighters eliminated." Said Lieutenant Commander Lee Oswald.

"Good work you guys." I say with praise.

Then Jaxina yells over the comms.

"Captain twenty more fighters just lit up in my heads up display, we can't fight them without shields what do we do now?"

"Make a run for It Jax, now!"

"Eye eye Captain."

Jaxina and I were no match for twenty fighters to take head on so we turned tail with the other two friendly support fighters and headed back to Lieutenant Commander Lee Oswald's squadron.

"Lee, we are inbound at hyper sonic velocity being pursued by four enemy squads get ready to engage," I order.

"Roger that, and get to safety Captain, Master Chief form up and engage long range missiles we will take out as many as we can before we have to switch to guns. Captain we got this."

Jaxina and I flew right past the friendly Firehawk squadron and once we were past and out of reach of the enemy fighters, Lee Oswald and his squad opens fire and the barrage of missiles rocket away and take out as many as was able and then the dog fight ensued shortly after.

PART THREE

FINAL THOUGHTS

THE ADMIRAL'S MEN GOT OUT matched by my squadron and the enemy got destroyed, we did lose a couple of fighters ourselves during the final battle but in the end we were victorious. We waited for more enemies to show themselves but none appeared. All in all I captured fourteen enemy I.R.F. Firehawk gunships and their pilots, not bad, although I would have liked to have captured the Admiral as well, it seems he managed to give us the slip once again, we did scan the asteroid belt numerous times but to no avail, he just disappeared.

We managed to tractor beam the immobilized gunships to the Supernova and throw the enemy pilots in the brigg. I will have to say that I don't like killing but in the end it became a do or die situation and luckily for me and my crew we came out of that situation alive.

It was reported to me later that the rescue of the colonists went well, Lieutenant Commander Lee Oswald, Lieutenant Leon Fernandez and Acting Sub Lieutenant Tyrel Johnson junior class found the mine the colonists were in. It was also reported that the conditions of the dank subterranean surface was unsafe. The small expansive cave held around two thousand people. Methane and high traces of carbon dioxide permeated the air. Thanks to the air conditioning units tying to pump clean air into the cave the smog wasn't lethal, it just made the people ill.

It was a well executed plan by Lieutenant Commander Lee Oswald and my team had no trouble leading the people to safety. The only problem they ran into was my Falcon class shuttle has only room for about fifteen people, so Lee requested a special conveyance from the Supernova.

Its like this, the Supernova is so large that the only way we can move cargo from the ship to the standard size docks most of the logistics centers around the galaxy have, is by what we call trucks. They are a type of a barge class freighter but not as large, they can hold up to a thousand people each because they are also twelve hundred meters long by six hundred meters wide and the Supernova has four. Only two trucks were needed to transport the colonists from Midas Eighty Eight to the Supernova and Cranky wasted no time in issuing the order while I was logging in some combat flight time with my wing-girl, Jaxina Bernardino.

The trucks require a special classification and only five members of my ships crew are rated to fly them. Acting Sub Lieutenant Don Watts, Sub Lieutenant Jaxina Bernardino and a couple of hangar bay crew, Junior Class Pilot Sergi Beltov and Junior Class Pilot Emily Danko. I'm the fifth pilot that's also rated to fly one. I still fly one because Don Watts the senior ships helms man refuses to fly one. It actually takes all four trucks to load and unload the Supernova and Jaxina always pilots the fourth truck.

This time the job fell to my Junior Class pilots Sergi Beltov and Emily Danko. Funny thing about them they have named their trucks as well and refuse to fly any other. Sergi's truck is known as the Bear and Emily's truck is known as the Bulldog. All two thousand colonists were rescued safely and brought on board the Supernova and were given medical treatment immediately. And wouldn't you know it five hundred people of the rescued colonists were actually non combatant crew from the I.R.F. Python as well. We now have a crew in the cryo engineering center and a lot nonunion maintenance personnel running around the ship fixing the glitches.

Even though the engineers from the warship have integrated themselves in engineering on the Supernova and know how to get our engine problem fixed they say we need a proper shipyard to do it in and the only place that was around at the time was the Pluto fuel depo and dry docks. A seedy colony full of scum and villainy if I ever saw one.

In the end we decided to carry on to Orion station, the station would be able to accommodate our repairs and fix the gaping hole that the Admiral caused to my beloved ship but it will be a long journey.

The media found out about the whole debacle at Midas Eighty Eight and when we finally arrived at Orion Station we were greeted with fan fare and considered heros. As for the prisoners they were arrested by the P.I.M.P.S. Yup that's right the P.I.M.P.S. They are the Planetary Intergalactic Magistrate Police Service, they call themselves arbitrators because really who wants to be known as a pimp which is what everybody in the galaxy calls them, we do, and I still think its funny.

I also found out that we barely escaped Midas Eighty Eight with our lives. You see after the colonists were rescued we went back to the I.R.F. Python to get the rest of the Firehawk gunships that were still on board and Lee wanted to finally raid the armoury. Also some of the Supernova's non commissioned crew that I brought with us went exploring the Python for salvage and they were the ones that discovered enough explosives rigged to the ship to cause a low yield nuclear explosion, and the clock was ticking.

Lee Oswald managed to procure enough weapons and armour to supply the entire crew of the Supernova. My ship now has a surplus of weapons and armour and no armoury to store them in. Needless to say we did not get all of the Firehawk gunships off the Python either we only managed to get about ten additional gunships before the warship went nuclear and destroyed the asteroid.

I think Admiral Victor Kruel has sent his message to the empire quite clearly, the empire has now declassified his profile and named him public enemy number one. The empire also has proposed a huge reward for any information that will lead to his capture and arrest.

On a lighter note the new crew members from the I.R.F. Python have fallen into their rolls very well and seem happy, now that we are at Orion Station its official I made them part of the crew of the Supernova and I'm their new Captain.

With that I'm going to sign off and head over to the casino and watch that new sport that everyone's raving about, the Monday night monkey knife fights with special guest commentators a Charleton Heston clone and Cornelius from the actual planet of the apes. Last week I heard that the Charleton Heston clone yelled at Cornelius and said. "Get your filthy paws off me you god damn dirty ape!" I hope says it again because that would be great.

Well until next time, I'm outta here, see ya.

The End.

Coming soon

Space Truckers

Volume Two

Waiting for a load

9 781956 349580